U0025454

The Garden Party and Sixpence

曼斯菲爾德
短篇小說選

原著 _ Katherine Mansfield
改寫 _ David A. Hill 譯者 _ 安卡斯

ABOUT THIS BOOK

For the Student

 Listen to the story and do some activities on your Audio CD.

 Talk about the story.

For the Teacher

Go to our Readers Resource site for information on using readers and downloadable Resource Sheets, photocopiable Worksheets, and Tapescripts. www.helblingreaders.com

For lots of great ideas on using Graded Readers consult Reading Matters, the Teacher's Guide to using Helbling Readers.

Structures

Sequencing of future tenses	• Could / was able to / managed to
Present perfect plus yet, already, just	• Had to / didn't have to
First conditional	• Shall / could for offers
Present and past passive	• May / can / could for permission
	• Might for future possibility
How long?	• Make and let
	• Causative have
Very / really / quite	• Want / ask / tell someone to do something

Structures from lower levels are also included.

CONTENTS

Katherine Mansfield Beaumont was born on October 14th 1888 in Wellington, New Zealand. She was the daughter of a middle-class colonial[1] family. She began writing when she was at school and her stories were published in two school magazines. In 1903, she moved to London to attend Queen's College, then in 1906 she returned to New Zealand. However, she found life very dull[2] after her time in London, and she persuaded[3] her father to let her return there with an allowance[4] of £100 a year.

She led a Bohemian[5] lifestyle until she moved to Germany[6] in 1909. In Germany she started writing in earnest[7] and in 1911, her first collection of stories *In a German Pension* was

published. She started writing for *Rhythm* magazine, and fell in love with its editor[8], John Middleton Murry. The couple eventually got married in 1918.

Katherine's life and work was changed by her brother's death in October 1915 in World War I. Many of her stories after his death focused[9] on children and her childhood memories. Katherine was friendly with both D H Lawrence and Virginia Woolf. Woolf said that Mansfield's was "the only writing I have ever been jealous of".

Katherine suffered[10] with ill health throughout her life. She was diagnosed[11] with tuberculosis[12] in 1918 and died of the disease[13] in 1923 when she was just 35. Katherine Mansfield is recognized as one of the greatest short story writers of the 20th century.

---

1 colonial [kə'lonjəl] (a.) 殖民地的
2 dull [dʌl] (a.) 乏味的
3 persuade [pə'swed] (v.) 說服
4 allowance [ə'lauəns] (n.) 零用錢
5 Bohemian [bo'himiən] (a.) 波希米亞的
6 Germany ['dʒɜmənɪ] (n.) 德國
7 earnest ['ɜnɪst] (n.) 熱忱

8 editor ['ɛdɪtə] (n.) 編輯
9 focus ['fokəs] (v.) 聚焦；集中
10 suffer ['sʌfə] (v.) 遭受
11 diagnose ['daɪəgnoz] (v.) 診斷
12 tuberculosis [tju,bɜkjə'losɪs] (n.) 結核病
13 disease [dɪ'ziz] (n.) 疾病

The Garden Party was written in the period after
Mansfield's brother's death in 1915 when the author
wrote a number of stories set in her native New
Zealand at the turn of the century. The scene of the
story – the Sheridan's large house and garden – is
clearly based on her family's opulent[1] home at 75
Tinakori Road in Wellington, where she lived from
1898 to 1903. The event – a middle-class garden party
– is also based on the kind of social occasions[2] she
would have taken part in[3] as a girl and young woman.

As the Sheridans prepare for the garden party, Laura,
their teenage[4] daughter learns that a neighboring
workman has died. The news disturbs[5] her and she feels
the party should be canceled[6] as a sign of respect. The
story is one of great contrasts[7] – the brightness, wealth[8]
and life at the party, and the darkness, poverty[9] and
death at the worker's house.

Sixpence tells the story of how the Bendall family's easygoing[10] and understanding attitude[11] to their lively son Dicky is suddenly overturned[12] when a visitor describes her own much more authoritarian[13] method of bringing up[14] her children. One small incident[15] will irreversibly[16] change the relationship between Mr. Bendall and his young son.

Both stories are fine examples of modernist[17] writing, showing how small incidents can have a profound[18] effect on the protagonists'[19] thoughts and actions.

1 opulent [ˈɑpjələnt] (a.) 富裕的
2 occasion [əˈkeʒən] (n.) 場合
3 take part in 參加
4 teenage [ˈtinˌedʒ] (a.) 十幾歲的
5 disturb [dɪsˈtɝb] (v.) 打擾；擾亂
6 cancel [ˈkænsl̩] (v.) 取消
7 contrast [ˈkɑnˌtræst] (n.) 對比；對照
8 wealth [wɛlθ] (n.) 財富
9 poverty [ˈpɑvɚtɪ] (n.) 貧窮
10 easygoing [ˈizɪˌgoɪŋ] (a.) 隨和的
11 attitude [ˈætətjud] (n.) 態度

12 overturn [ˌovɚˈtɝn] (v.) 顛覆；推翻
13 authoritarian [əˌθɔrəˈtɛrɪən] (a.)
   權威式的
14 bring up 養育
15 incident [ˈɪnsədn̩t] (n.) 事件
16 irreversibly [ˌɪrɪˈvɝsəbl̩ɪ] (adv.)
   不可逆轉的
17 modernist [ˈmɑdɚnɪst] (n.) 現代派
18 profound [prəˈfaʊnd] (a.) 深刻的
19 protagonist [proˈtægənɪst] (n.)
   主人翁

1 Think of your house. Imagine you are walking through it, describe the rooms and the feeling you get from each individual room.

2 Look at these scenes from the story. Discuss with a partner.

a) Describe the scenes.
b) What is the atmosphere like in each one?
c) Who do you think lives there?

3 Now write a short description of each one. Imagine you live there. Describe your home.

4 What is the best party you have ever been to?
What made it so good?
What did you do there?
Who went to the party?

5 Look at the following list of parties. With a partner discuss
what you expect to happen at each one. How are they
different from each other? What would you wear to each one?

[a] Your younger brother/sister's birthday party
[b] Your best friend's birthday party
[c] A dinner party
[d] A tea party
[e] A garden party
[f] A fancy dress party
[g] A theme party

6 Choose one of the events above. Plan it. Think of times,
food, entertainment and dress code.

7 Now design an invitation card for the party.

Come to My Spot Party

Friday 23rd March
From Seven O'clock

And don't forget . . .
. . . you must wear something spotty!

The Garde

Party

The weather was ideal. There could not have been a more perfect day for a garden party. Windless[1], warm, the sky without a cloud. And the blue was thinly covered with a haze[2] of light gold, as it is sometimes in early summer. The gardener had been up since dawn, cutting the lawns[3] and sweeping[4] them, until the grass seemed to shine. As for the roses, you could not help feeling they understood that roses are the only flowers that impress people at garden parties; the only flowers that everybody is certain of knowing. Hundreds, yes, literally[5] hundreds, had come out in a single night; the green bushes bowed down[6] as though they had been visited by angels.

Breakfast was not over before the men came to put up the big tent.

"Where do you want the marquee[7] put, mother?"

"My dear child, it's no use asking me. I'm determined to leave everything to you children this year. Forget I am your mother. Treat me as an honored guest. "

But Meg could not possibly go and supervise the men. She had washed her hair before breakfast, and sat drinking her coffee with a green towel round her head, and a dark wet curl stuck onto each cheek. Jose, the butterfly, came down in a silk petticoat[8] and a kimono jacket.

Think

- Try to imagine the garden.
- Think of a place outdoors that you like. Describe it.

---

1 windless ['wɪndlɪs] (a.) 無風的
2 haze [hez] (n.) 薄霧
3 lawn [lɔn] (n.) 草坪
4 sweep [swip] (v.) 打掃
5 literally ['lɪtərəlɪ] (adv.) 不加誇張地

6 bow down 低垂
7 marquee [mɑrˈki] (n.) 大營帳
8 petticoat ['pɛtɪ,kot] (n.) 婦女所穿的襯裙

🎧 "You'll have to go, Laura; you're the artistic one."

Off Laura went, still holding her piece of bread and butter. It's so delicious to have an excuse for eating outside and, besides, she loved having to arrange things; she always felt she could do it so much better than anybody else.

Four men wearing shirts stood grouped together[1] on the garden path. They carried poles covered with rolls of canvas and they had big tool bags on their backs. They looked impressive[2]. Laura wished now that she was not holding that piece of bread and butter, but there was nowhere to put it and she couldn't possibly throw it away. She blushed[3] and tried to look severe and even a little bit short-sighted[4] as she came up to them.

"Good morning," she said, copying her mother's voice. But it sounded so awful that she was ashamed, and hesitated, like a little girl,

"Oh – erm – have you come – is it about the marquee?"

"That's right, miss," said the tallest of the men, and he moved his tool bag, pushed back his straw hat and smiled down at her. "That's it."

His smile was so easy, so friendly, that Laura recovered. What nice eyes he had – small, but such a dark blue! And now she looked at the others, they were smiling too. "Cheer up, we won't bite," their smile seemed to say. How very nice workmen were! And what a beautiful morning! She mustn't mention the morning; she must be business-like.

---

1 group together 站在一塊兒
2 impressive [ɪmˋprɛsɪv] (a.) 予人深刻
　印象的
3 blush [blʌʃ] (v.) 臉紅
4 short-sighted [ˋʃɔrtˋsaɪtɪd] (a.) 近視的

5 stare [stɛr] (v.) 盯；凝視
6 frown [fraʊn] (v.) 皺眉
7 it will hit you in the eye
　可以讓你注意到
8 scan [skæn] (v.) 掃視

🎧 "Well, what about the lily-lawn? Would that do?"

And she pointed to the lily-lawn with the hand that didn't hold the bread and butter. They turned and stared[5] in that direction. A little fat man pushed his lower lip out and the tall one frowned[6].

"I don't like it," he said. "You wouldn't notice it. You see, with a thing like a marquee" – and he turned to Laura in his easy way – "you want to put it somewhere where it will hit you in the eye[7], if you understand what I mean."

"A corner of the tennis court," she suggested. "But the band's going to be in one corner."

"H'm, going to have a band, are you?" said another of the workmen. He was pale. He had a tired look as his eyes scanned[8] the tennis court. What was he thinking?

"Only a small band," said Laura gently. Perhaps he wouldn't mind so much if the band was quite small. But the tall man interrupted.

"Look here, miss, that's a fine place. Against those trees. Over there. That'll do fine."

Against the karakas[1]. Then the karaka trees would be hidden. And they were so lovely, with their broad, gleaming[2] leaves, and their clusters[3] of yellow fruit. They were like the trees you imagined growing on a desert island – proud, solitary, lifting their leaves and fruit to the sun in a kind of silent splendor. Must they be hidden by a big tent? They must. Already the men had shouldered[4] their poles and were going there. Only the tall man was left.

He bent down and pinched[5] some lavender leaves, put his thumb and finger to his nose and sniffed[6] the scent. When Laura saw him do that she forgot all about the karakas in her wonder at him caring for small things like that – caring for the smell of lavender. How many of the men that she knew would have done such a thing?

Oh, how extraordinarily nice workmen were, she thought.

Why couldn't she have workmen for friends rather than the silly boys she danced with and who came to Sunday night supper? She would get on much better with men like these. It's all the fault, she decided, as the tall man drew something on the back of an envelope, of these absurd class distinctions. Well she didn't feel them. Not a bit, not an atom.

1 karakas [kəˈrækəs] (n.) 卡拉卡樹（一 種熱帶植木）
2 gleaming [ˈglimɪŋ] (a.) 油油發亮的
3 cluster [ˈklʌstɚ] (n.) 簇；群
4 shoulder [ˈʃoldɚ] (v.) 肩起
5 pinch [pɪntʃ] (v.) 擰
6 sniff [snɪf] (v.) 嗅聞

And now there came the chock-chock of wooden hammers. Someone whistled, someone called out, "Are you all right there, matey[1]?" "Matey!" The friendliness of it! Just to prove how happy she was, just to show the tall man how comfortable she felt with them, how she despised[2] stupid conventions, Laura took a big bite of her bread and butter as she stared at his little drawing. She felt just like a workgirl.

Think

- How does Laura react to the workmen?
- What are 'class distinctions'?
- Why does Laura say they are 'absurd'?

"Laura, Laura, where are you? Telephone, Laura!" a voice called from the house.

"Coming!" Away she skimmed[3], over the lawn, up the path, up the steps, across the veranda[4] and into the porch[5]. In the hall her father and Laurie were brushing their hats, ready to go to the office.

"I say, Laura," said Laurie very fast, "you might just have a look at my coat before this afternoon. See if it needs pressing[6]."

"I will," she said. Suddenly she couldn't stop herself. She ran over to Laurie and gave him a small, quick squeeze. "Oh, I do love parties, don't you?" she gasped[7].

1 matey [ˈmetɪ] (n.) 〔口〕朋友
2 despise [dɪˈspaɪz] (v.) 鄙視
3 skim [skɪm] (v.) 飛躍而過
4 veranda [vəˈrændə] (n.) 遊廊
5 porch [portʃ] (n.) 門廊
6 press [prɛs] (v.) 熨燙

7 gasp [gæsp] (v.) 喘氣
8 rather [ˈræðɚ] (adv.) 〔口〕的確
9 dash [dæʃ] (v.) 急奔
10 old girl 親愛的（親暱用法）
11 delighted [dɪˈlaɪtɪd] (a.) 愉快的
12 fling [flɪŋ] (v.) 急伸

"*Rather*[8]," said Laurie's warm, boyish voice, and he squeezed his sister too, and gave her a gentle push. "Dash[9] off to the telephone, old girl[10]."

The telephone. "Yes, yes; oh yes. – Kitty? Good morning, dear. Come to lunch? Do, dear. Delighted[11], of course. It will only be a very simple meal – just sandwich crusts and broken meringues and what's left over. Yes, it's a perfect morning! Your white? Oh, I certainly should. One moment – hold the line. Mother's calling." And Laura sat back. "What, mother? Can't hear!"

Mrs. Sheridan's voice came floating down the stairs. "Tell her to wear that sweet hat she had on last Sunday."

"Mother says you're to wear that sweet hat you had on last Sunday. Good. One o'clock. Bye-bye."

Laura put back the telephone, flung[12] her arms over her head, took a deep breath, stretched and let them fall. "Huh," she sighed, and sat up quickly. She stood still, listening. All the doors in the house seemed to be open. The house was alive with soft, quick steps and running voices. The green cloth-covered door that led[13] to the kitchen swung[14] open and shut with a soft thud[15]. And now there came a long, strange sound. It was the heavy piano being moved on its stiff[16] little wheels.

But the air! If you stopped to notice, was the air always like this? Little light winds were playing chase, coming in at the tops of the windows, going out at the doors. And there were two tiny spots of sun, one on the inkpot[17], one on a silver photograph frame, playing too. Darling little spots. Especially the one on the inkpot lid. It was quite warm. A warm little silver star. She could have kissed it.

---

13 lead [lid] (v.) 通向
14 swing [swɪŋ] (v.) 擺動
15 thud [θʌd] (n.) 重擊聲
16 stiff [stɪf] (a.) 不靈活的
17 inkpot [ˈɪŋkˌpɑt] (n.) 墨水瓶

Think

- Why does Laura want to kiss the inkpot lid?
- Think of a time that something you saw made you feel very happy.
- Share with a partner.

The front door bell rang and Sadie's skirt rustled[1] on the stairs. A man's voice murmured[2]; Sadie answered, careless, "I'm sure I don't know. Wait. I'll ask Mrs. Sheridan."

"What is it, Sadie?" Laura came into the hall.

"It's the florist, Miss Laura."

It was indeed. There, just inside the door, stood a wide, shallow[3] tray full of pink lilies. No other kind. Nothing but lilies – canna lilies, big pink flowers, wide open, radiant, almost frighteningly alive on bright crimson[4] stems.

"O-oh, Sadie!" said Laura, and the sound was like a little moan[5]. She bent down as if to warm herself at that bright mass[6] of lilies; she felt they were in her fingers, on her lips, growing inside her.

"It's some mistake" she said faintly[7]. "Nobody ever ordered so many. Sadie, go and find Mother." But at that moment Mrs. Sheridan joined them.

---

1 rustle ['rʌsl̩] (v.) 沙沙作響
2 murmur ['mɝmɚ] (v.) 低聲説
3 shallow ['ʃælo] (a.) 淺的
4 crimson ['krɪmzn̩] (a.) 深紅色的
5 moan [mon] (n.) 嗚咽聲

6 mass [mæs] (n.) 塊；群
7 faintly ['fentlɪ] (adv.) 微弱地
8 interfere [ˌɪntɚ'fɪr] (v.) 介入；干涉
9 pile [paɪl] (v.) 堆積

"It's quite right," she said calmly. "Yes, I ordered them. Aren't they lovely?" She pressed Laura's arm. "I was passing the shop yesterday, and I saw them in the window. And I suddenly thought that for once in my life I shall have enough canna lilies. The garden party will be a good excuse."

"But I thought you said you didn't want to interfere[8]," said Laura.

Sadie had gone. The florist's man was still outside, by his van. She put her arm round her mother's neck and gently, very gently, bit her mother's ear.

"My darling child, you wouldn't like a logical mother, would you? Don't do that. Here's the man."

He carried even more lilies, another whole tray.

"Pile[9] them up, just inside the door, on both sides of the porch, please," said Mrs. Sheridan. "Don't you agree, Laura?"

"Oh, I do, Mother."

In the drawing-room Meg, Jose and good little Hans had at last succeeded in moving the piano.

"Now, if we put this sofa against the wall and move everything out of the room except the chairs, don't you think?"

"Yes."

"Hans, move these tables into the smoking-room, and bring a sweeper to take these marks off the carpet and – one moment, Hans – " Jose loved giving orders to the servants and they loved obeying her. She always made them feel as if they were taking part in some drama. "Tell mother and Miss Laura to come here at once."

"Very good, Miss Jose."

She turned to Meg. "I want to hear what the piano sounds like, just in case I'm asked to sing this afternoon. Let's try 'This Life is Weary[1]'."

Pom! Ta-ta-taa Tee-ta! The piano burst out[2] so passionately that Jose's face changed. She clasped[3] her hands. She looked mournfully[4] and enigmatically[5] at her mother and Laura as they came in.

This life is *Wee*-ary,
A Tear – a Sigh.
A Love that *Chan*-ges,
This life is *Wee*-ary,
A Tear – a Sigh.
A Love that *Chan*-ges,
And then . . . Goodbye!

1 weary [ˋwɪrɪ] (a.) 疲倦的
2 burst out 突然爆發
3 clasp [klæsp] (v.) 緊握；扣緊
4 mournfully [ˋmɔrnflɪ] (adv.) 悲傷地
5 enigmatically [ˌɛnɪgˋmætɪkl̩ɪ] (adv.)
　　讓人捉摸不透地

But at the word 'Goodbye', although the piano sounded more desperate than ever, her face broke into a brilliant, dreadfully[1] unsympathetic smile.

"Aren't I in good voice, mummy?" she beamed[2].

This life is *Wee*-ary,
Hope comes to Die.
A Dream – a *Wa*-kening.

But now Sadie interrupted them.

"What is it, Sadie?"

"If you please, madam, cook asks if you have got the flags[3] for the sandwiches?"

"The flags for the sandwiches, Sadie?" echoed Mrs. Sheridan dreamily. And the children knew by her face that she hadn't got them.

"Let me see." And she said to Sadie firmly, "Tell cook I'll let her have them in ten minutes."

Sadie went.

"Now, Laura," said her mother quickly, "come with me into the smoking room. I've got the names somewhere on the back of an envelope. You'll have to write them out for me. Meg, you go upstairs this minute and take that wet towel off your head. Jose, run and finish dressing this instant. And – and, Jose, pacify[4] cook if you go into the kitchen, will you? I'm terrified of her this morning."

🎧 The envelope was found at last behind the dining-room clock, though how it got there Mrs. Sheridan could not imagine.

"One of you children must have stolen it out of my bag, because I remember vividly⁵ – cream-cheese with lemon curd⁶. Have you done that?"

"Yes."

"Egg and – " Mrs. Sheridan held the envelope away from her. "It looks like mice. It can't be mice, can it?"

"Olive," said Laura, looking over her shoulder.

"Oh, yes of course, olive. What a horrible combination it sounds. Egg and olive."

They were finished at last, and Laura took them off to the kitchen. She found Jose there pacifying the cook, who did not look at all terrifying.

"I've never seen such exquisite sandwiches," said Jose's rapturous⁷ voice. "How many kinds did you say there were, cook? Fifteen?"

"Fifteen, Miss Jose."

"Well, cook, I congratulate you."

Cook swept up crusts with the long sandwich knife, and smiled broadly.

"Godber's has come", announced Sadie, coming out of the pantry.

---

1 dreadfully [ˈdrɛdfəlɪ] (adv.) 可怕地
2 beam [bim] (v.) 愉快地微笑
3 flag [flæg] (n.) 標籤；旗子
4 pacify [ˈpæsəˌfaɪ] (v.) 撫慰
5 vividly [ˈvɪvɪdlɪ] (adv.) 鮮活地
6 curd [kɜd] (n.) 凝乳狀食品
7 rapturous [ˈræptʃərəs] (a.) 興奮的

That meant the cream puffs[1] had come. Godber's were famous for their cream puffs. Nobody thought of making them at home.

"Bring them in and put them on the table, my girl," ordered cook.

Sadie brought them in and then went back to the door. Of course Laura and Jose were much too grown-up to really care about such things. All the same, they couldn't help agreeing that the puffs looked very attractive. Very. Cook began arranging them, shaking off the extra icing sugar[2].

"Don't they take you back to[3] all our parties?" said Laura.

"I suppose they do," said practical Jose, who never liked to be carried back. "They look beautifully light and feathery, I must say."

"Have one each, my dears," said cook in her comfortable voice. "Your mother won't know."

Oh impossible. Special cream puffs so soon after breakfast. The very idea made you shudder[4].

All the same, two minutes later Jose and Laura were licking their fingers with that absorbed inward[5] look that can only come after eating cream.

"Let's go into the garden, out the back way," suggested Laura. "I want to see how the men are getting on with the marquee. They're such awfully[6] nice men."

Think

- Imagine what Laura and Jose are thinking as they are eating the cream puffs.
- What foods remind you of when you were a child?

But the door was blocked by cook, Sadie, Godber's man and Hans. Something had happened.

"Tuk-tuk-tuk," clucked[7] cook, like an agitated hen. Sadie had her hand holding her cheek as though she had toothache. Hans' face was puzzled[8] in the effort to understand. Only Godber's man seemed to be enjoying himself. It was his story.

"What's the matter? What's happened?"

"There's been a horrible accident," said cook. "A man killed."

"A man killed! Where? How? When?"

But Godber's man wasn't going to have his story snatched[9] from under his nose.

"Know those little cottages[10] just down here, miss?" Know them? Of course she knew them. "Well, there's a young man living there, name of Scott, a carter[11]. His horse jumped up at the sound of an engine, corner of Hawke Street this morning, and he was thrown down on the back of his head. Killed."

"Dead!" Laura stared at Godber's man.

"Dead when they picked him up," said Godber's man, enjoying it. "They were taking the body home as I came up here." And he said to the cook, "He's left a wife and five little ones."

"Jose, come here." Laura caught hold of her sister's sleeve and dragged[12] her through the kitchen to the other side of the green door. Then she paused and leaned[13] against it.

---

1 puff [pʌf] (n.) 泡芙
2 icing sugar 糖霜
3 take you back to 使想起
4 shudder [ˈʃʌdɚ] (v.) 戰慄
5 inward [ˈɪnwəd] (a.) 向內心的
6 awfully [ˈɔfʊlɪ] (adv.)〔口〕非常
7 cluck [klʌk] (v.) 發咯咯聲

8 puzzled [ˈpʌzḷd] (a.) 困惑的
9 snatch [snætʃ] (v.) 奪走
10 cottage [ˈkɑtɪdʒ] (n.) 農舍；小屋
11 carter [ˈkɑrtɚ] (n.) 駕駛貨車者
12 drag [dræg] (v.) 拖
13 lean [lin] (v.) 傾斜

"Jose!" she said, horrified, "however are we going to stop everything?"

"Stop everything, Laura!" cried Jose in astonishment. "What do you mean?"

"Stop the garden party, of course." Why did Jose pretend?

But Jose was still more amazed. "Stop the garden party? My dear Laura, don't be so absurd. Of course we can't do anything of the kind. Nobody expects us to. Don't be so extravagant."

"But we can't possibly have a garden party with a man dead just outside the front gate."

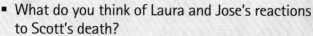

Think

- What do you think of Laura and Jose's reactions to Scott's death?
- What would you have wanted to do?

That really was extravagant, for the little cottages were in a lane[1] to themselves at the very bottom of the hill that led up to the house. A wide road ran between. True, they were far too near. They were extremely ugly and had no right to be in the neighborhood at all. They were poor little white-washed[2] buildings. In the gardens there was nothing but cabbage stalks[3], sick hens and tomato cans. Even the smoke coming out of their chimneys was poor. Little rags[4] of smoke, so unlike the great silvery plumes[5] that uncurled[6] from the Sheridans' chimneys.

Washerwomen lived in the lane, and sweeps[7] and a cobbler[8] and a man whose house-front was covered all over with tiny birdcages.

Children were everywhere. When the Sheridans were little they were forbidden to go there because of the terrible language and of what diseases they might catch.

But since they had grown up Laura and Laurie sometimes passed through on their walks. It was disgusting and dirty. They came out with a shudder. But still you had to go everywhere; you had to see everything. So through they went.

"And just think of what a band would sound like to that poor woman," said Laura.

"Oh, Laura!" Jose began to be seriously annoyed. "If you're going to stop a band playing every time someone has an accident, you'll lead a very difficult life. I'm every bit as sorry about it as you. I feel just as sympathetic." Her eyes hardened. She looked at her sister just as she used to when they were little and fighting together. "You won't bring a drunken[9] workman back to life by being sentimental," she said softly.

"Drunk! Who said he was drunk?" Laura turned ferociously[10] on Jose. She said just as they had used to say on these occasions, "I'm going straight up to tell Mother."

"Do, dear," cooed[11] Jose.

---

1 lane [len] (n.) 巷
2 white-washed [ˈhwaɪtˈwɑʃt] (a.) 漆白色的
3 stalk [stɔk] (n.) 莖；葉柄
4 rag [ræg] (n.) 破布；碎布
5 plume [plum] (n.) 羽毛
6 uncurl [ʌnˈkɝl] (v.) 變直
7 sweep [swip] (n.) 掃煙囪的人
8 cobbler [ˈkɑblɚ] (n.) 補鞋匠
9 drunken [ˈdrʌŋkən] (a.) 酒醉的
10 ferociously [fəˈroʃəslɪ] (adv.) 兇猛地
11 coo [ku] (v.) 柔情地低聲說話

"Mother, can I come into your room?" Laura turned the big glass doorknob[1].

"Of course, child. Why, what's the matter? What's given you such a color?" And Mrs. Sheridan turned round from her dressing table. She was trying on a new hat.

"Mother, a man's been killed," began Laura.

"Not in the garden?" interrupted her mother.

"No, no!"

"Oh, what a fright you gave me!" Mrs. Sheridan sighed with relief and took off the big hat and held it on her knees.

Think

- Why is Mrs. Sheridan relieved?
- What do you think of her reaction?

"But listen, Mother," said Laura. Breathless, half choking[2], she told the dreadful story. "Of course, we can't have our party, can we?" she pleaded[3]. "The band and everybody are arriving. They'd hear us, Mother; they're nearly neighbors!"

To Laura's astonishment her mother behaved just like Jose; it was harder to bear[4] because she seemed amused. She refused to take Laura seriously.

"But, my dear child, use your common sense. It's only by accident that we've heard of it. If someone had died there normally – and I can't understand how they keep alive in those tiny little holes – we would still have our party, wouldn't we?"

Laura had to say "yes" to that, but she felt it was all wrong. She sat down on her mother's sofa and pinched the edge of the cushion.

"Mother, isn't it really terribly heartless[5] of us?" she asked.

"Darling!" Mrs. Sheridan got up and came over to her carrying the hat. Before Laura could stop her she had popped[6] it on.

"My child!" said her mother, "the hat is yours. It's made for you. It's much too young for me. I have never seen you look such a picture. Look at yourself!" And she held up her hand-mirror.

"But, Mother," Laura began again. She couldn't look at herself; she turned aside.

This time Mrs. Sheridan lost patience just as Jose had done.

"You are being very absurd, Laura," she said coldly. "People like that don't expect sacrifices from us. And it's not very sympathetic to spoil[7] everyone's enjoyment as you're doing now."

"I don't understand," said Laura, and she walked quickly out of the room into her own bedroom. There, quite by chance, the first thing she saw was this charming[8] girl in the mirror, in her black hat trimmed with daisies and a long black velvet ribbon.

---

1 doorknob [`dor,nɑb] (n.) 球形門把
2 choke [tʃok] (v.) 哽噎
3 plead [plid] (v.) 懇求
4 bear [bɛr] (v.) 忍受

5 heartless [`hɑrtlɪs] (a.) 冷酷無情的
6 pop [pɑp] (v.) 突然迅速地一放
7 spoil [spɔɪl] (v.) 破壞
8 charming [`tʃɑrmɪŋ] (a.) 迷人的

Never had she imagined she could look like that. Is Mother right? she thought. And now she hoped her mother was right. Am I just being extravagant? Perhaps it was extravagant. Just for a moment she had another glimpse[1] of that poor woman and those little children and the body being carried into the house. But it all seemed unclear, unreal, like a picture in the newspaper. I'll remember it again after the party's over, she decided. And somehow that seemed quite the best plan.

Lunch was over by half-past one. By half-past two they were all ready for the party. The green-coated band had arrived and was set up[2] in a corner of the tennis court.

"My dear!" trilled[3] Kitty Maitland, "aren't they too like frogs for words? You should have arranged them around the pond with the conductor in the middle on a leaf."

Laurie arrived from work and waved to them on his way to dress for the party. At the sight of him Laura remembered the accident again. She wanted to tell him. If Laurie agreed with the others, then it was bound to[4] be all right. And she followed him into the hall.

"Laurie!"

"Hallo!" He was half-way upstairs, but when he turned round and saw Laura he suddenly puffed[5] out his cheeks and stared at her. "My word[6], Laura! You look wonderful," said Laurie. "What an absolutely beautiful hat!"

---

1 glimpse [glɪmps] (n.) 一瞥
2 set up 準備
3 trill [trɪl] (v.) 用顫音說話
4 be bound to 一定會……
5 puff [pʌf] (v.) 使膨脹
6 My word! 哇！（用以表示驚嘆）

Laura said faintly "Is it?" and smiled up at Laurie, and didn't tell him after all.

Soon after that people began coming in streams[1]. The band started to play; the hired[2] waiters ran from the house to the marquee. Wherever you looked there were couples strolling[3], bending down to smell flowers, greeting, moving on over the lawn. They were like bright birds that had landed in the Sheridans' garden for this one afternoon, on their way to – where? Ah, what happiness it is to be with people who are all happy, to press hands, to press cheeks, smile into eyes.

"Darling Laura, how well you look!"

"How that hat suits you, child!"

"Laura, you look quite Spanish. I've never seen you look so striking[4]."

And Laura, glowing[5], answered softly, "Have you had tea? Won't you have an ice-cream? The passion-fruit ices are rather special." She ran to her father and begged him: "Daddy darling, can't the band have something to drink?"

And the perfect afternoon slowly ripened[6], slowly faded[7], slowly its petals closed.

Think

- What metaphor does the author use here for the passing of time?
- How do you imagine time?

Laura helped her mother with the goodbyes. They stood side by side in the porch until it was all over.

"All over, all over, thank heaven," said Mrs. Sheridan. "Round up[8] the others, Laura. Let's go and have some fresh coffee. I'm exhausted. Yes, it's been very successful. But oh, these parties, these parties! Why do you children insist on giving parties!"

And they all of them sat down in the deserted[9] marquee.

"Have a sandwich, daddy dear. I wrote the flag."

"Thanks." Mr. Sheridan took a bite and the sandwich was gone.

"I suppose you didn't hear of a beastly[10] accident that happened today?" he said.

"My dear," said Mrs. Sheridan, holding up her hand. "We did. It nearly ruined the party. Laura insisted we should put it off."

"Oh, mother!" Laura didn't want to be teased[11] about it.

"It was a horrible business all the same," said Mr. Sheridan. "The man was married too. Lived just below us in the lane, and leaves a wife and half a dozen[12] children, so they say."

An awkward silence fell. Mrs. Sheridan played with her cup. Really, it was very tactless[13] of father . . .

---

1 in streams 連續不斷
2 hired [haɪrd] (a.) 受雇的
3 stroll [strol] (v.) 散步
4 striking [ˋstraɪkɪŋ] (a.) 驚為天人的
5 glowing [ˋgloɪŋ] (a.) 容光煥發的
6 ripen [ˋraɪpən] (v.) 進入巔峰
7 fade [fed] (v.) 枯萎

8 round up 召集
9 deserted [dɪˋzɝtɪd] (a.) 空蕩無人的
10 beastly [ˋbistlɪ] (a.) 可怕的
11 tease [tiz] (v.) 取笑
12 dozen [ˋdʌzn] (n.) 一打
13 tactless [ˋtæktlɪs] (a.) 不識相的

Suddenly she looked up. There on the table were all those sandwiches, cakes, puffs, all uneaten, all going to be wasted. She had one of her brilliant ideas. "I know," she said. "Let's fill up a basket. Let's send that poor woman some of this perfectly good food. At any rate it will be the greatest treat for the children. Don't you agree? And she's sure to have neighbors calling in and so on[1]. What a good thing to have it all already prepared. Laura!" She jumped up. "Get me the big basket out of the cupboard."

"But, mother, do you really think it's a good idea?" said Laura.

Again, how strange, she seemed to be different from them all. To take scraps[2] from the party. Would the poor woman really like that?

"Of course! What's the matter with you today? An hour or two ago you were insisting on us being sympathetic." Oh well! Laura ran for the basket. It was filled; it was heaped[3] by her mother.

"Take it yourself, darling," she said. "Run down just as you are. No, wait. Take the arum lilies[4], too. People of that class are so impressed by arum lilies."

"The stems will ruin[5] her dress," said practical Jose.

So they would. Just in time. "Only the basket, then. And Laura" – her mother followed her out of the marquee – "don't . . . "

---

1 and so on 諸如此類
2 scrap [skræp] (n.) 碎片；小塊
3 heap [hip] (v.) 堆積
4 arum lily [ˈɛrəm ˈlɪlɪ] 海芋
5 ruin [ˈruɪn] (v.) 毀壞

"What, mother?"

No, better not put such ideas into the child's head!

"Nothing! Run along."

Think

- What do you think Mrs. Sheridan was going to say to Laura?
- Why did she stop herself?
- Do you think it's a good idea to take the left-over party food to the dead man's house?

It was just growing dusky[1] as Laura shut the garden gates. A big dog ran by like a shadow. The road shone white, and down in the valley the little cottages were in deep shadow. How quiet it seemed after the afternoon. Here she was going down the hill to somewhere where a man lay dead, and she couldn't realize it. Why couldn't she? She stopped a minute. And it seemed to her that kisses, voices, tinkling[2] spoons, laughter, the smell of crushed[3] grass were somehow inside her. She had no room[4] for anything else. How strange! She looked up at the pale sky, and all she thought was, "Yes, it was the most successful party."

Now the wide road was crossed. The lane began, smoky and dark. Women in shawls and men's caps hurried by. Men hung over fences; the children played in the doorways. A low hum[5] came from the poor little cottages. In some of them there was a flicker[6] of light, and a shadow moved across the window.

Laura bent her head and hurried on. She wished now she had put on a coat. How her dress shone! And the big hat with the velvet ribbon – if only it was another hat! Were the people looking at her? They must be. It was a mistake to have come; she knew all along it was a mistake. Should she go back even now? No, too late. This was the house. It must be. A dark group of people stood outside. Beside the gate an old, old woman with a crutch[7] sat in a chair, watching. She had her feet on a newspaper.

1 dusky [ˈdʌskɪ] (a.) 暗淡的
2 tinkling [ˈtɪŋklɪŋ] (a.) 鏗鏘響的
3 crushed [krʌʃt] (a.) 被壓踏的
4 room [rum] (n.) 空間
5 hum [hʌm] (n.) 嗡嗡聲
6 flicker [ˈflɪkɚ] (n.) 閃爍；搖曳
7 crutch [krʌtʃ] (n.) 丁形柺杖

25 The voices stopped as Laura drew near. The group parted. It was as though[1] she was expected, as though they had known she was coming here.

Laura was terribly nervous. Pushing the velvet ribbon over her shoulder, she said to a woman standing by, "Is this Mrs. Scott's house?" and the woman, smiling strangely, said. "It is, my lass[2]."

Oh, to be away from this! She actually said, "Help me, God," as she walked up the tiny path and knocked. To be away from those staring eyes, or to be covered up in anything, one of those women's shawls even. I'll just leave the basket and go, she decided. I won't even wait for it to be emptied.

Think

How does Laura feel in the lane, and why?
What does she want to do?
How do you think you would have felt in her place?

1 as though 彷彿
2 lass [læs] (n.) 小姑娘

Then the door opened. A little woman in black showed in the dark.

Laura said, "Are you Mrs. Scott?"

But to her horror the woman answered, "Walk in, please, miss," and she was shut in the passage[1].

"No," said Laura, "I don't want to come in. I only want to leave this basket. Mother sent – "

The little woman in the dark passage seemed not to have heard her. "Step this way, please, miss," she said in an unpleasant voice, and Laura followed her.

She found herself in a poor little low kitchen, lighted by a smoky lamp. There was a woman sitting in front of the fire.

"Em," said the little woman who had let her in. "Em! It's a young lady." She turned to Laura. She said, "I'm 'er[2] sister, miss. You'll excuse 'er, won't you?"

"Oh, but of course!" said Laura. "Please, please don't disturb her. I – I only want to leave – "

But at that moment the woman at the fire turned round. Her face, puffed up[3], red, with swollen[4] eyes and swollen lips, looked terrible. She seemed as if she couldn't understand why Laura was there. What did it mean? Why was this stranger standing in the kitchen with a basket? What was it all about? And the poor face started crying again.

"All right, my dear," said the other. "I'll thank the young lady."

And she began again, "You'll excuse her, miss, I'm sure," and her face, swollen too, tried to smile.

---

1 passage [ˈpæsɪdʒ] (n.) 通道；走廊
2 'er 即「her」
3 puff up 浮腫
4 swollen [ˈswolən] (a.) 腫脹的
5 'im 即「him」
6 brush past 經過時輕輕碰觸了一下

Laura only wanted to get out, to get away. She was back in the passage. The door opened. She walked straight through into the bedroom, where the dead man was lying.

"You'd like to look at 'im[5], wouldn't you?" said Em's sister, and she brushed past[6] Laura over to the bed. "Don't be afraid, my lass" – and now her voice sounded fond[7] and sly[8], and fondly she pulled down the sheet – " 'e[9] looks a picture. There's nothing to show. Come along, my dear."

Laura came.

There lay a young man, fast asleep – sleeping so soundly, so deeply, that he was far, far away from them both. Oh, so remote, so peaceful. He was dreaming. Never wake him up again. His head was sunk in the pillow, his eyes were closed; they were blind under the closed eyelids. He was lost in his dream. What did garden parties and baskets and lace dresses mean to him? He was far away from all those things. He was wonderful, beautiful. While they were laughing and while the band was playing, this marvel had come to the lane.

"Happy . . . happy . . . All is well," said that sleeping face. "This is just as it should be. I am content." But all the same you had to cry, and she couldn't go out of the room without saying something. Laura gave a loud childish sob[10].

"Forgive my hat," she said. And this time she didn't wait for Em's sister. She found her way out of the door, down the path past all those dark people.

---

7 fond [fɑnd] (a.) 溫柔的　9 'e 即「he」
8 sly [slaɪ] (a.) 詭祕的　10 sob [sɑb] (n.) 嗚咽聲

At the corner of the lane she met Laurie.

He stepped out of the shadow. "Is that you, Laura?"

"Yes."

"Mother was getting anxious[1]. Was it all right?"

"Yes, quite, Oh, Laurie!" She took his arm, she pressed up against him.

"I say, you're not crying, are you?" asked her brother.

She shook her head. She was.

Laurie put his arm around her shoulder. "Don't cry," he said in his warm, loving voice. "Was it awful?"

"No," sobbed Laura. "It was simply marvelous. But Laurie – " She stopped; she looked at her brother. "Isn't life," she hesitated, "isn't life –" But she couldn't explain what life was. No matter. He quite understood.

"Isn't it, darling?" said Laurie.

Think

- Is Laura's reaction to the dead man what you expected?
- Why/why not?
- What do you think Laura wanted to say about life at the end?

---

1 anxious [ˈæŋkʃəs] (a.) 擔心的

Ⓐ Personal Response

1 What did you think of the story? Write a paragraph describing your response.

2 What did you think of the ending? Were you surprised? Why do you think Laura reacted in this way?

3 What does the story say about class relations?

4 What does it tell us about the lives of the rich and the poor at that time?

Ⓑ Comprehension

5 Tick T (true) or F (false) below.

T F ⓐ The action of the story takes place on one day.

T F ⓑ All the action takes place at the Sheridan's house.

T F ⓒ Mrs. Sheridan wants to look after all the arrangements.

T F ⓓ There are four Sheridan children.

T F ⓔ Laura's sister Meg disagrees with her about stopping the party.

T F ⓕ Mr. Sheridan and Laurie go to work in the morning.

T F ⓖ Laurie reminds the family about Scott's death later.

T F ⓗ Laura is terrified when she sees the dead body.

T F ⓘ Laura can't explain her feelings to her brother.

6 Look at the words in the box. Which of them refer to the Sheridan's house and garden, and which to the workers' cottages and lane?

> smoky   alive   dark   sun   poor   warm
>
> shadow   bright   happy   ugly   disgusting   perfect

7 Make two columns, and then explain how the words above in each column are related, and how they are different to the words in the other column.

The Sheridan's House/Garden	The Workers' Cottages/Lane
alive	smoky

❸ Characters

8 There are four groups of characters in this story.
Complete the table below with the missing information.

GROUP	PERSON	FACTS ABOUT THEM
The Sheridan family and their friends	① Mr. Sheridan	
	②	
	③	The main character in the story.
	④	
	⑤	
	⑥	Works in an office with his father.
	⑦	
The Sheridans' servants	⑧ Sadie	
	⑨	The person who prepares most of the food.
	⑩	
	⑪ The Gardener	
People who deliver things for the party or who are hired to work at it	⑫ 4 workmen	
	⑬ The florist	
	⑭	Tells about Scott's death.
	⑮	They wear green uniforms and play the music.
	⑯ Hired waiters	
People in the worker's cottage	⑰	The carter who was killed in an accident.
	⑱ Em Scott	
	⑲ The other woman	

9 Form groups of four. Each person picks one person from one of the groups above. Introduce yourself, describe your part in the story and say what you notice and think about what is going on. Say whether you think the Sheridans should have canceled the garden party because of the death.

10 Describe Laura's reactions

- a) When she meets the workmen who are putting up the marquee.
- b) When she finds out about Scott's death.
- c) When her mother gives her the hat.
- d) At the end of the party.
- e) When she is walking towards the dead man's house.
- f) When she goes into the house.
- g) When she is walking home with Laurie.

11 How are the three sisters described? How do you imagine them?

12 What do the following quotes tell us about Mrs. Sheridan?

- a) "My dear child, it's no use asking me. I'm determined to leave everything to you children this year." (page 13)
- b) "Not in the garden?" (page 30)
- c) "People like that don't expect sacrifices from us. And it's not very sympathetic to spoil everyone's enjoyment as you're doing now." (page 31)
- d) "Let's fill up a basket. Let's send that poor woman some of this perfectly good food. At any rate it will be the greatest treat for the children." (page 36)

13 Find quotes that tell us about Laura's character. What is your favorite one? Discuss with a partner.

14 Imagine you are Mrs. Sheridan. Write a diary entry for the day of the garden party.

❶ Plot and theme

15 Katherine Mansfield is a Modernist writer. She uses a variety of literary techniques throughout the story.

- ⓐ *stream-of-consciousness* to show the character's actual thoughts directly.
- ⓑ direct speech
- ⓒ indirect speech
- ⓓ author narration of events
- ⓔ author comment on character.

Look at the following extract from page 26, which has been broken up into separate lines. Decide which of the literary techniques (a) to (e) above is being used in each extract.

_____	ⓐ	Sadie brought them in and went back to the door
_____	ⓑ	Of course Laura and Jose were much too grown-up to care about such things.
_____	ⓒ	All the same, they couldn't help agreeing that the puffs looked very attractive. Very.
_____	ⓓ	Cook began arranging them, shaking off the extra icing sugar.
_____	ⓔ	"Don't they take you back to all our parties?" said Laura.
_____	ⓕ	"I suppose they do," said practical Jose, who never liked to be carried back
_____	ⓖ	"They look beautifully light and feathery, I must say."
_____	ⓗ	"Have one each, my dears," said cook in her comfortable voice. "Your mother won't know."
_____	ⓘ	Oh impossible. Special cream puffs so soon after breakfast. The idea made you shudder.

16 With a partner discuss the effect of each of these techniques.

17 "The central theme of the story is how people develop when confronted by new situations." How does Laura develop as a person throughout the story?

18 Fill in the following list:

The Garden Party is a short story about

a

b

c

d

e

19 Share your list in groups of three or four, adding any ideas you think are important.

20 Death, and its effect on Laura, is one of the main themes in *The Garden Party*. Think of how her attitude to death changes throughout the story.

a On hearing the news of Scott's death

b During the party

c When she goes into the dead man's house

d When she leaves the house

21 At the end why does she say that going to the dead man's house was "simply marvelous"?

Sixpence

1 Look at the illustration. Describe the boy. What is he doing? What do you think he is like? Use adjectives from the box below.

> active   angry   excited   foolish   friendly
> lazy   naughty   quiet   shy   unfriendly

2 What happens next? Choose one of the options below.

_____ [a] The boy's mother arrives and takes the knife and plate from him.

_____ [b] The boy throws the plate at his sisters.

_____ [c] The boy puts the knife and plate down.

_____ [d] The boy drops the plate.

3 Imagine you are one of his sisters. With a partner imagine what you say to persuade him to put the plate down. What does he reply?

4 Were you naughty when you were a small child? Did you do anything to make your parents angry?

5 Did your parents punish you if you did something wrong as a small child? If so, how did they punish you?

6 How do your parents react now if you do something they don't agree with?

7 Which of the following do you think is worse? Discuss in groups of four.

_____ a Ignoring what your parents say.
_____ b Going out when you know you shouldn't.
_____ c Not doing your homework.
_____ d Telling lies to cover up for a friend.
_____ e Doing or saying something rude.
_____ f Ignoring someone you know.

8 Have you ever apologized to anyone for something you did? What did you say? How did you feel?

9 Has anyone ever apologized to you? What did they say? How did your feelings towards them change after the apology?

Children are difficult to understand. Why does a small boy like Dicky – usually as good as gold[1], sensitive, affectionate[2], obedient, and marvelously sensible for his age – have moods[3] when, without the slightest warning, he suddenly went "mad dog," as his sisters called it, and nothing could be done with him?

"Dicky, come here! Come here, boy, at once! Do you hear your mother calling you? Dicky!"

But Dicky wouldn't come. Oh, he heard, right enough[4]. A clear little laugh was his only reply. And away he ran; hiding, running through the uncut grass on the lawn, hurrying past the woodshed[5], making a rush for the kitchen garden, staring at his mother from behind the apple-tree trunks, and jumping up and down like a wild animal.

It all started at tea-time. Dicky's mother and Mrs. Spears, who was spending the afternoon with her, were quietly sitting and sewing in the drawing room. The children were eating their bread and butter as nicely and quietly as you please, and the servant girl had just poured out the milk and water, when Dicky suddenly seized[6] the bread plate, put it upside down on his head, and clutched[7] the bread knife.

"Look at me!" he shouted.

---

1 good as gold 非常好
2 affectionate [əˈfɛkʃənɪt] (a.) 溫柔親切的
3 moods [mudz] (n.)〔複數形〕喜怒無常
4 right enough 當然（加強語氣）
5 woodshed [ˈwʊd.ʃɛd] (n.) 柴房
6 seize [siz] (v.) 抓住
7 clutch [klʌtʃ] (v.) 攫取

His startled[1] sisters looked, and before the servant girl could get there, the bread plate wobbled[2], slid, slipped to the floor, and broke into small pieces. At this awful point the little girls lifted up their voices and shrieked[3] their loudest.

"Mother, come and look what he's done!"

"Dicky's broken a great big plate!"

"Come and stop him, Mother!"

Can you imagine how mother came running? But she was too late. Dicky had jumped out of his chair, run through the French windows on to the veranda[4], and, well – there she stood – helpless.

What could she do? She couldn't chase after the child. She couldn't hunt for Dicky through the apple and plum trees. That would be too undignified[5]. It was more than annoying; it was exasperating[6]. Especially as Mrs. Spears, Mrs. Spears of all people, whose two boys were so good, was waiting for her in the drawing room.

"Very well, Dicky," she cried, "I shall have to think of some way of punishing you."

"I don't care," sounded a high little voice, and again there was that ringing[7] laugh. The child was behaving very strangely.

Think

- Why do you think Dicky behaved as he did?
- What were you like as a child?

"Oh, Mrs. Spears, I don't know how to apologize for leaving you by yourself like this."

"It's quite all right, Mrs. Bendall," said Mrs. Spears, in her soft, sugary voice. She seemed to smile to herself. "These little things will happen from time to time. I only hope it is nothing serious."

"It was Dicky," said Mrs. Bendall, looking rather helplessly for her only fine needle[8]. And she explained the whole thing to Mrs. Spears. "And the worst of it is, I don't know how to cure[9] him. When he's in that mood, nothing seems to have the slightest effect on him."

Mrs. Spears opened her pale eyes. "Not even a beating[10]?" she said.

But Mrs. Bendall, threading[11] her needle, said: "We have never beaten the children. The girls never seem to have needed it. And Dicky is such a baby, and the only boy. Somehow . . . "

"Oh, my dear," said Mrs. Spears, and she laid[12] her sewing down. "I am not surprised Dicky has these little outbreaks[13]. You don't mind my saying so? But I'm sure you make a great mistake in trying to bring up children without beating them. Nothing really takes its place. And I speak from experience, my dear. I used to try gentler ways."

---

1 startled [ˈstɑrtld] (a.) 受到驚嚇的
2 wobble [ˈwɑbl] (v.) 搖晃
3 shriek [ʃrik] (v.) 尖叫
4 veranda [vəˈrændə] (n.) 遊廊
5 undignified [ʌnˈdɪgnəˌfaɪd] (a.) 沒尊嚴的
6 exasperating [ɪgˈzæspəˌretɪŋ] (a.) 使人惱怒的
7 ringing [ˈrɪŋɪŋ] (a.) 銀鈴聲般的

8 needle [ˈnidl] (n.) 針
9 cure [kjʊr] (v.) 對治
10 beating [ˈbitɪŋ] (n.) 打
11 thread [θrɛd] (v.) 穿 (針)
12 lay [le] (v.) 置放
13 outbreak [ˈaʊtˌbrek] (n.) 爆發

Mrs. Spears drew in her breath with a little hissing sound – "soaping[1] the boys' tongues, for instance, with yellow soap, or making them stand on the table for the whole of Saturday afternoon. But no, believe me," said Mrs. Spears, "there is nothing, there is nothing like handing them over[2] to their father."

Mrs. Bendall, deep inside, was dreadfully shocked to hear about the yellow soap. But Mrs. Spears seemed to take it as a normal thing, so she did too.

"Their father," she said. "Then you don't beat them yourself."

"Never." Mrs. Spears seemed quite shocked at the idea. "I don't think it's the mother's job to beat the children. It's the duty of the father. And, besides, he impresses[3] them so much more."

"Yes, I can imagine that," said Mrs. Bendall faintly.

"Now my two boys," Mrs. Spears smiled kindly, encouragingly, at Mrs. Bendall, "would behave just like Dicky if they were not afraid to. As it is . . . "

"Oh, your boys are perfect little models," cried Mrs. Bendall.

They were. Quieter, better-behaved little boys, in the presence of grown-ups, could not be found. In fact, Mrs. Spears' visitors often made the remark that you would never think that there was a child in the house. There wasn't – very often.

In the front hall, under a large picture of fat, happy old monks fishing by the riverside, there was a thick, dark horsewhip[4] that had belonged to Mr. Spears' father. And for some reason the boys preferred to play out of sight[5] of this, behind the dog kennel or in the tool house, or round about the dustbin.

Think

- Do Mrs. Spears' children seem relaxed and happy? Why/why not?

---

1 soap [sop] (v.) 以肥皂清先
2 hand sb over to sb 把某人
　交給某人處理
3 impress [ɪmˋprɛs] (v.) 給予很大的影響
4 horsewhip [ˋhɔrsˌhwɪp] (n.) 馬鞭
5 out of sight 目所不見之處

"It's such a mistake," sighed Mrs. Spears, breathing softly, as she folded her work, "to be weak with children when they are little. It's such a sad mistake, and one so easy to make. It's so unfair to the child. That is what one has to remember. Now Dicky's behavior this afternoon seemed to me as though he had done it on purpose[1]. It was the child's way of showing you that he needed beating."

"Do you think so?" Mrs. Bendall was a weak little woman, and this impressed her very much.

"I do; I feel sure of it. And a sharp reminder[2] now and then," cried Mrs. Spears in quite a professional way, "given by the father, will save you so much trouble in the future. Believe me, my dear." She put her dry, cold hand over Mrs. Bendall's.

"I shall speak to Edward the moment he comes in," said Dicky's mother firmly.

Think

- Do you agree with Mrs. Spears' ideas about punishment? Why/why not?

1 on purpose 故意地
2 reminder [rɪˋmaɪndɚ] (n.) 提醒物
3 stagger [ˋstægɚ] (v.) 蹣跚而行
4 tired out 非常累

5 brim [brɪm] (n.) 突出的（帽）緣
6 cabinet [ˋkæbənɪt] (n.) 櫥；櫃
7 grin [grɪn] (v.) 露齒而笑

The children had gone to bed before the garden gate banged and Dicky's father staggered[3] up the concrete steps carrying his bicycle. It had been a bad day at the office. He was hot, dusty, and tired out[4].

But by this time Mrs. Bendall had become quite excited over the new plan, and she opened the door to him herself.

"Oh, Edward, I'm so thankful you have come home," she cried.

"Why, what's happened?" Edward lowered the bicycle and took off his hat. A red mark showed where the brim[5] had pressed his head. "What's up?"

"Come – come into the drawing room," said Mrs. Bendall, speaking very fast. "I simply can't tell you how naughty Dicky has been. You have no idea – you can't have, being at the office all day – how a child of that age can behave. He's been simply dreadful. I have no control over him – none. I've tried everything, Edward, but it's all no use. The only thing to do," she finished breathlessly, "is to beat him – is for you to beat him, Edward."

In the corner of the drawing room there was a cabinet[6], and on the top shelf stood a brown china bear with a painted tongue. It seemed in the shadow to be grinning[7] at Dicky's father, to be saying, "Hooray, this is what you've come home to!"

"But why on earth[1] should I start beating him?" said Edward, staring at the bear. "We've never done it before."

"Because," said his wife, "don't you see, it's the only thing we can do. I can't control the child . . . " Her words flew from her lips. They rang round him, rang round his tired head. "We can't possibly afford[2] a nurse. The servant girl has more than enough to do. And his naughtiness is beyond words. You don't understand, Edward; you can't, you're at the office all day."

The bear poked[3] out his tongue. The angry voice went on. Edward sank into a chair.

"What am I to beat him with?" he said weakly.

"Your slipper, of course," said his wife. And she knelt down to untie his dusty shoes.

"Oh, Edward," she wailed[4], "you've still got your cycling clips[5] on in the drawing room. No, really – "

"Here, that's enough." Edward nearly pushed her away. "Give me that slipper."

Think

- How does Edward feel when he gets home?
- What does his wife do that makes him feel worse?
- Why does he decide to beat Dicky?

---

1 on earth 究竟
2 afford [əˋford] (v.) 供得起
3 poke [pok] (v.) 探出
4 wail [wel] (v.) 嚎啕
5 cycling clip 騎自行車時
用來束長褲褲腳的金屬環

He went upstairs. He felt like a man in a dark net. And now he wanted to beat Dicky. Yes, he wanted to beat something. My God, what a life! The dust was still in his hot eyes. His arms felt heavy.

He pushed open the door of Dicky's tiny room. Dicky was standing in the middle of the floor in his nightclothes. At the sight of him, Edward's heart gave a warm throb[1] of rage[2].

"Well, Dicky, you know what I've come for," said Edward.

Dicky made no reply.

"I've come to give you a beating."

No answer.

"Lift up your nightclothes."

At that Dicky looked up. He flushed[3] deep pink. "Must I?" he whispered.

"Come on, now. Be quick about it," said Edward, and then, holding the slipper tight, he hit Dicky hard three times.

"There, that'll teach you to behave properly[4] to your mother."

Dicky stood there, hanging his head.

"Look sharp[5] and get into bed," said his father.

Still he did not move. But a shaking voice said, "I've not cleaned my teeth yet, Daddy."

"Eh, what's that?"

Dicky looked up. His lips were quivering[6] but his eyes were dry. He hadn't made a sound or cried. Only he swallowed and said quietly, "I haven't cleaned my teeth, Daddy."

1 throb [θrɑb] (n.) 跳動　　4 properly [`prɑpəlɪ] (adv.) 恰當地

2 rage [redʒ] (n.) 狂怒　　5 look sharp　趕快

3 flush [flʌʃ] (v.) 臉紅　　6 quiver [`kwɪvə] (v.) 顫抖；發抖

But at the sight of that little face Edward turned, and, not knowing what he was doing, he ran from the room, down the stairs, and out into the garden. Good God! What had he done? He walked along and hid in the shadow of the pear tree by the hedge. Beaten Dicky – beaten his little son with a slipper – and what for? He didn't even know.

Dicky's father groaned and held onto the hedge. And he didn't cry. Never a tear. If only he'd cried or got angry. But that "Daddy"! And again he heard the quivering whisper. Forgiving like that without a word. But he'd never forgive himself – never. Coward[1]! Fool! Brute[2]! And suddenly he remembered the time when Dicky had fallen off his knee and sprained[3] his wrist while they were playing together. He hadn't cried then, either. And that was the little hero he had just beaten.

Think

- How does Edward feel about beating Dicky? Why?
- How do you think Dicky feels?

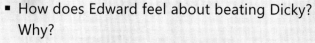

1 coward [ˈkaʊəd] (n.) 懦夫
2 brute [brut] (n.) 殘暴的人；畜生
3 sprain [spren] (v.) 扭傷
4 fringe [frɪndʒ] (n.) 鬚邊
5 plain [plen] (adv.) 清楚地

6 kneel down 跪下
7 beg [bɛg] (v.) 懇求
8 awkward [ˈɔkwəd] (a.) 笨拙的
9 lash [læʃ] (n.) 眼睫毛

Something's got to be done about this, thought Edward. He walked quickly back to the house, up the stairs, into Dicky's room. The little boy was lying in bed. In the half-light his little head, with the square fringe[4], showed plain[5] against the pale pillow. He was lying quite still, and even now he wasn't crying. Edward shut the door and leaned against it. What he wanted to do was to kneel down[6] by Dicky's bed and cry and beg[7] to be forgiven. But, of course, he couldn't do that sort of thing. He felt awkward[8], and his heart pained him.

"Not asleep yet, Dicky?" he said lightly.

"No, Daddy."

Edward came over and sat on his boy's bed, and Dicky looked at him through his long lashes[9].

"Nothing the matter, is there?" said Edward, half whispering.

"No-o, Daddy," came from Dicky.

Edward put out his hand, and carefully he took Dicky's hot little hand.

"You – mustn't think any more of what happened just now, little man," he said quietly. "See? That's all over now. That's forgotten. That's never going to happen again. See?"

"Yes, Daddy."

"So the thing to do now is to feel better, my boy," said Edward, "and to smile." And he tried himself to give a weak smile. "To forget all about it – to – eh? Little man . . . Old boy[1] . . . "

Dicky lay as before. This was terrible. Dicky's father jumped up and went over to the window. It was nearly dark in the garden. The servant girl had run out, and she was taking some white clothes off the bushes and was putting them over her arm. But in the wide sky the evening star shone, and the big tree, black against the pale light, moved its leaves softly. All this he saw, while he felt in his trouser pocket for his money. Bringing it out, he chose a new sixpence and went back to Dicky.

"Here you are, my boy. Buy yourself something," said Edward softly, laying the sixpence on Dicky's pillow.

But could even that – could even a whole sixpence – remove what had been?

Think

- Why does Edward give Dicky sixpence?
- How do you think Dicky feels about it?

---

1 little man; old boy 對小男孩的親暱稱法

Ⓐ Personal Response

1 What did you think of the story? Write a paragraph describing your response.

2 What did you think of the father's reaction at the end? Do you think he acted correctly? Why/why not?

3 What would you have done in the same situation?

4 What do you think Dicky is thinking at the end of the story?

5 Do you think the story has a moral? If so, what is it?

❸ Comprehension

6 What does Dicky Bendall do to annoy his mother?

7 What does he do immediately after he is naughty?

_____ a He goes to his room.

_____ b He starts crying.

_____ c He runs out into the garden.

_____ d He apologizes.

8 Why does his mother not punish him immediately?

9 Mrs. Spears tells Mrs. Bendall about three ways she punished her boys. List them and say which one she thought was best.

a _____

b _____

c _____

10 How does Mrs. Bendall react to what Mrs. Spears says? Does she tell Mrs. Spears what she thinks?

11 How has she dealt with Dicky before when he was naughty?

12 What happens when Mr. Bendall comes home from the office?

13 What is the significance of the "brown china bear"?
How does it make Mr. Bendall feel?

14 Has Mr. Bendall ever beaten his son before?

15 Why does he decide to beat Dicky now? Tick.

_____ (a) Because Dicky is naughty and needs to be punished.

_____ (b) Because he feels trapped and frustrated.

_____ (c) Because he has tried other ways to discipline Dicky and they haven't worked.

16 How does he feel after he has beaten Dicky?
Choose adjectives from the box below.

> angry confused guilty happy relaxed
> relieved satisfied tired worried

17 What does he remember from the past?
How does this add to the way he is feeling?

Ⓒ Characters

18 Read this extract:

> "What could she do? She couldn't chase after the child. She couldn't hunt for Dicky through the apple and plum trees. That would be too undignified. It was more than annoying; it was exasperating. Especially as Mrs. Spears, Mrs. Spears of all people, whose two boys were so good, was waiting for her in the drawing room."

What insights does it give into the character of Mrs. Bendall? Underline words or expressions that tell you about what she is like.

19 Mrs. Bendall is described as a "weak little woman". How do you think she is weak? In pairs find examples.

20 What is Mrs. Bendall's mood like when her husband comes in? How does she treat him?

21 What happens when Mrs. Bendall notices her husband's cycling clips? What does this tell us about her? How does he react?

22 What do you think Mr. Bendall is hoping for when he gets home? Does he find it?

23 Read from where Edward Bendall comes home to where he goes to beat Dicky (pages 63-66). Make a list of all the words and phrases which are used to describe Edward and how he felt. What impression do they give of him?

24 After the beating, Mr. Bendall goes back to his son's room. What does he want to do, and why doesn't he do it?

25 Imagine you are Mr. Bendall. Describe your day. Say what happened and explain why. Say how you felt as each thing happened.

26 Work in pairs. Write the conversation Mr. and Mrs. Bendall have later that evening about the beating. Try to bring out their different opinions and feelings. Act it out in front of the class.

27 'Dicky is just a normal boy'. Look through the texts for positive and negative aspects of Dicky's behavior.

POSITIVE	NEGATIVE

28 Which character do you feel most sympathetic towards? Give reasons.

❶ Plot and theme

29 One of the themes of the story is how people change their usual behavior when their ideas or beliefs are challenged.

How are Mr. and Mrs. Bendall's usual behavior and beliefs challenged? How do they change? Write a paragraph about each one, using quotations from the text.

30 How does Mr. Bendall get to know himself better in the story? How does he develop? What limitations does he find?

31 Each of the characters carries out one main action that affects the rest of the story. Write what they do and the consequences their action has.

Who?	What does s/he do?	What are the consequences of this action?
Dicky		
Mrs. Spears		
Mrs. Bendall		
Mr. Bendall		

32 Read the last two lines of the story:

> "Here you are, my boy. Buy yourself something,"
> said Edward softly, laying the sixpence on
> Dicky's pillow. But could even that – could
> even a whole sixpence – remove what had been?

Is there a definite resolution? What conclusions can you draw at the end of the story? What do you think Mansfield feels about what happened?

33 Katherine Mansfield, like other modernist writers, often uses a carefully described detail of an object to give the whole impression of the atmosphere of a place or the feelings of a person. Find an example of this in *Sixpence*.. What object does she choose? How does the object describe the atmosphere of the moment and the character's feelings?

34 Fill in the following list:

Sixpence is a short story about

a _____

b _____

c _____

d _____

e _____

Use these details to help you write a summary of the story.

35 Why do you think the author chose the title *Sixpence*.? What is the significance of the 'sixpence' in the story? Do you like the title?

作者簡介　凱瑟琳・曼斯菲爾德，1888 年 10 月 14 日出生於紐西蘭的威靈頓，出身於一個中產階級的殖民者家庭。她在學生時代便開始創作，還曾在兩份學校期刊上發表過小說。 1903 年，她搬到倫敦，在皇后學院念書，到了 1906 年才又回到紐西蘭。從倫敦回來之後，她不太能適應紐西蘭單調的生活，最後她說服父親每年給她一百鎊的生活費，讓她回到倫敦。

她在倫敦時過著居無定所的生活，一直到了 1909 年，她搬到德國，才開始積極寫作。 1911 年，她出版了第一本小說集《在德國公寓》。她也開始為《Rhythm》雜誌寫小說，並且和雜誌社的編輯 John Middleton Murry 相戀，兩人後來於 1918 年結婚。

1915 年 10 月，她的弟弟於第一次世界大戰中喪生，這件事情改變了她的生活和寫作。弟弟過世後，她的很多小說轉而以兒童和兒時回憶為主。D. H. 勞倫斯和維吉尼亞・吳爾夫都和她有不錯的交情，吳爾夫曾說，曼斯菲爾德的創作，「是唯一不會讓我心生嫉妒的作品」。

凱瑟琳一生多病。1918 年，她被診斷出罹患肺結核，1923 年，死於肺結核，年僅 35 歲。凱瑟琳公認是 20 世紀一位偉大的短篇小說作家。

本書簡介　《花園派對》是在凱瑟琳的弟弟於 1915 年去世後那段時間所寫的。那時凱瑟琳寫的幾個故事背景都設定在紐西蘭家鄉，講述世紀交替那個年代的故事。《花園派對》這個故事的場景——榭里丹家的豪宅和花園——顯然是以她自己的家為雛型，那是一棟座落在威靈頓提那克里路 75 號的大房子，她於 1898 年到 1903 年居住於此。故事中的事件——一個中產階級家庭舉辦的一場花園派對——也是作者在兒童和少年時代常會見到的社交場面。

就在榭里丹家忙著張羅花園派對之際，年少的女兒蘿拉得知住家旁邊有一個工人往生了。這件事讓她感到不安，她覺得應該取消派對，以示尊重。這個故事做了一個強烈的對照——派對上一派光鮮亮麗、尊貴奢華、生氣勃勃，相對於工人家中的黑暗、貧窮和死亡。

《六便士銅板》講的則是班道家的事，班道家對他們調皮的兒子弟奇，一向比較溫和包容，但時當一位訪客說出自己如何對孩子嚴家管教之後，班道家對兒子的態度就有了一百八十度的轉變。後來發生了一件小事情，讓班道先生和兒子的關係，就此產生了變化。

上述這兩個故事，是很典型的現代小說，描繪出一個小小的件事，會如何深刻地影響到故事人物的想法和行為。

花園派對

P.13

這種天氣再恰當不過了，正是舉辦花園派對的大好時光。風和日麗，萬里無雲，蔚藍的天空泛著一層薄薄的金光，這是初夏偶爾可見的風光。園丁在天破曉時就起床幹活了，他修剪草坪，清掃乾淨，一片綠茵看起來閃閃發光。說到玫瑰花，你不禁會覺得這戶人家很懂得在花園派對中，只有玫瑰花才能讓人留下印象，這是唯一人人都知道的花。這些數百朵的玫瑰花，確實是有數百朵之多，它們在一夕之間綻放開來；綠色的樹叢躬下腰來，彷彿在恭迎這些降臨的天使一般。

這家人還在用早餐，等著工人來搭架大棚子。

「媽，你想大棚子要架在哪裡比較好？」

「我的寶貝孩子，這不用問我。我已經決定了，今年什麼事都由你們小孩來發落。忘了我是你媽吧，把我當成一位貴客就好。」

梅格無法去監督工人，她在吃早餐之前才洗過頭髮。她坐在那裡啜著咖啡，頭上纏著一條綠毛巾，兩頰還探出兩捲濕濕的黑髮。喬絲，這隻花枝招展的花蝴蝶，她穿著一件絲質的襯裙、披著睡袍走過來。

思索一下
• 想像一下花園的樣子。
• 想出一個你喜歡的戶外地點，並加以形容。

P.14

「蘿拉，你去監工吧，你是最有美感的。」

蘿拉於是出發，手上還拿著一塊奶油麵包。只怪麵包太美味，就容她拿著它離餐桌吧。再說，她是很喜歡布置東西，她自認為，在這方面別人是遠遠不及她的。

在花園的小徑上，有四個穿著襯衫的工人圍攏站在一起。他們扛著用帆布包捲起來的竿子，背上背著一個偌大的工具袋，架勢十足。蘿拉頓時但願自己手上沒有拿著奶油麵包，但麵包沒地方擱，又不能扔掉。她覺得很窘，便刻意裝出一副正經的樣子，然後帶著她一點點的近視眼，走向工人。

「早啊！」她模仿媽媽的講話語調，但聲音聽起來卻很彆扭，像個小女孩一樣

怯怯懦懦的。

「哦，那個……你們來……是要搭棚子的嗎？」

「是的，小姐。」個頭最高的工人說道。他挪了一下工具包，把草帽往後推，低下頭對她笑笑，說道：「沒錯。」

蘿拉發現他的笑容很自在、很友善。他有一雙漂亮的眼睛，小小的，是湛藍色的！她又看看其他的工人，工人們也都對她笑了笑，那些笑容彷彿在對她說：「開心點，我們又不會咬人。」他們每一個人都那麼友善！今天這個早上，何其美好！但她不能聊這個，她得擺出雇主的樣子。

P.15

「搭在百合花圃那邊？合適嗎？」

她用沒有拿麵包的那隻手，指向百合花圃，工人朝著手指的方向望過去。其中一個略顯福態的工人嘟出下嘴唇，那個高個子工人則是皺起眉頭。

「我覺得不太好，位置不夠明顯。你想，像棚子這樣的東西，」高個子用他那種悠然的態度，轉向蘿拉說：「應該要搭在比較醒目的地方，你懂我的意思吧！」

她建議道：「網球場的角落比較醒目，但那裡是樂隊的位置。」

「哦，你們要請樂隊來？」另一個工人說道。他臉色蒼白，用有氣無力的表情望了望網球場，不知道心裡在打什麼主意。

P.16

「是一個小小的樂隊啦。」蘿拉輕聲地答道。樂隊是大是小，工人應該也無所謂。這時高個子插話進來。

「小姐，你看那裡，那裡不錯，就在林子的對面，在那裡，那裡很適合。」

那個地方在卡拉卡樹的對面，這樣就會把樹遮住。這些樹很漂亮，有油亮亮的寬闊葉片和一叢叢黃色的果子。這種樹的外型，好比想像中孤島上會有的那種樹──昂然孤挺，樹葉和果子高高地舉向太陽，給人一種靜肅的感覺。一定要用大棚子把這些樹擋在後面嗎？勢在必行了，因為工人們已經扛著竿子逕自走過去，只有高個子還待在原地。

P.17

他彎下腰，搓了搓薰衣草的葉子，然後將指頭湊近鼻頭，嗅一嗅花香。蘿拉看著這一幕，卡拉卡樹的事頓時被拋在腦後；她很驚訝，這個男人怎麼會留心這種小事情，竟然會喜歡薰衣草的味道。在她認識的男人當中，又有幾個會做這種事？

她心想，哇，這些工人真是很不一樣。

她怎麼不交交這種工人朋友，何必淨跟那些會跟她跳舞，然後週日晚上才會過來吃頓晚飯的笨蛋男生做朋友？眼前這些男人好相處多了。高個子在一個信封袋的背面畫東西，她琢磨著：都嘛是因為可笑的階級區別，真是大錯特錯了。她呢，可是一點階級意識都沒有的，一丁點兒都沒有。

P.18

這時，傳來了木槌的叩叩聲。有人在吹哨子，有人喊道：「老兄，你那裡沒事吧？」「老兄！」真有人情味啊！蘿拉一邊看著高個子畫畫，一邊對著奶油麵包大咬一口，以表現自己的快意，並且讓高個子知道，她跟他們在一起很自在，而且她對那些愚蠢的禮俗很不以為然。她感到自己也化身成工人了。

思索一下

・面對工人，蘿拉有何反應？
・什麼是「階級區別」？
・為什麼蘿拉說階級區別「很可笑」？

「蘿拉，蘿拉，你在哪裡？電話，蘿拉！」屋子裡傳來聲音。

「來囉！」她一路快步跑著。她跳過草坪，走上小徑，躍上階梯，通過陽台，轉進走廊。大廳裡，父親和勞瑞正在刷著他們的帽子，準備去上班。

「我說蘿拉啊，你在今天下午以前幫我檢查一下我的外套，看需不需要燙一下。」勞瑞很快地說道。

「好。」蘿拉說罷，身子一時來不及停住，就撞上了勞瑞，輕輕地擠了他一下。「我是很喜歡派對啦，你呢？」她氣喘吁吁地說道。

P.19

「我很喜歡啊！」勞瑞用他還帶著稚氣的溫暖聲音說道，然後也擠了妹妹一下，輕輕地推了推她。「老姑娘，快去接電話吧！」

電話中。「你好，是，哦，是凱蒂嗎？早啊，親愛的，要過來吃午餐嗎？來嘛，親愛的。當然啦，可開心的了。午餐很簡單，就一些三明治片、酥皮捲，和一些剩下的食物。很好啊，今天早上太棒了！妳那個白色的？哦，我會的。等一下，不要掛電話，我媽在叫我。」蘿拉坐了下來，喊道：「媽，什麼事情？我聽不到你！」

榭里丹夫人的聲音沿著樓梯傳了下來。「跟她說，要她戴她上星期天戴的那頂漂亮的帽子。」

「媽媽要你戴你上星期天戴的那頂漂亮的帽子。很好。一點鐘。再見。」

蘿拉掛上電話，她兩手往後抱住腦後勺，深呼吸了一下，接著將兩手伸展了

83

一下，然後放下。「哎。」她嘆了口氣，接著很快地打直身子。她靜靜坐著，聽著各種聲響。屋子的門應該都是打開的，屋子裡有輕快的腳步聲和此起彼落的說話聲，一派生氣盎然。有人大手推開廚房那道蓋著綠布的門，門在關起來時輕輕地砰了一聲。接著傳來一個長長的奇怪聲響，那是沉重的鋼琴被移動的聲音，琴腳上拖著不靈活的小輪子。

看看空氣！留意一下空氣，這就是空氣的風貌嗎？從窗戶上方進來的微風互相追逐著，然後又從門扉那裡跑出去。空氣中還有兩個小小的光點，一個在墨水瓶，一個在銀色的相框，兩個光點閃爍不已。小光點很吸引人，尤其是墨水瓶蓋子上的光點，很暖和，像一顆溫暖的銀色小星星，讓她不禁想親吻下去。

P.20

思索一下

• 為什麼蘿拉會想親吻墨水瓶的蓋子？
• 回想一下，你是否曾經因為看到什麼，而讓你心情變得很好？
• 跟你的朋友分享一下。

前門的門鈴響起，紗荻走下樓梯，裙擺窣窣地作響著。外頭傳來男人嗡嗡的講話聲，紗荻漫不經心地答道：「我很確定我不知道，你等等，我去問一下榭里丹夫人。」

「紗荻，是誰啊？」蘿拉走進大廳。

「蘿拉小姐，是送花的。」

可不呢，門口內放了一個大大的淺盤，上面滿滿的都是粉紅色的花，而且清一色都是美人蕉──大朵大朵的粉紅色美人蕉，它們恣情地綻放著，芬芳吐豔，在鮮亮的赭色莖幹上顯得生氣勃勃。

「哦，紗荻！」蘿拉用略帶哀怨的語氣說道。她蹲下身，像是要跟那一大盤鮮艷的美人蕉取暖似的。她用手指和嘴唇去感受這些花朵，她感到這些花是長在她的內心世界裡的。

她低聲地說：「一定是搞錯了，哪有人會訂這麼多花。紗荻，你去找我媽。」說時巧，榭里丹夫人這時已經走過來了。

P.21

「沒有搞錯，這是我訂的。」夫人鎮靜地說：「這些花很漂亮吧？」她握住蘿拉的手臂，說道：「我昨天經過花店，在櫥窗看到這些花時，我突然有一個想法，我想說，我這一生，好歹要有這麼一次，可以擁有好多好多的美人蕉。這次的花園派對，剛好就是一個大好時機。」

「我還以為你説你這次都要放手不管事了呢。」蘿拉説。

這時紗荻已經離開，送花的人還站在外頭的貨車旁。蘿拉伸手輕輕環住媽媽的脖子，微微地齧了一下媽媽的耳朵。

「我的小寶貝，你不喜歡媽媽太理智，對吧？別這樣，送花的人走過來了。」

他捧來了另一整盤花，比剛剛那盤還大。

「把花堆起來，就放在門的裡面這邊，請沿著門廊的兩邊放。蘿拉，你覺得這樣放好嗎？」榭里丹夫人説。

「很好啊，媽。」

P.22

在客廳裡，梅格、喬絲和乖巧的小漢斯終於把鋼琴的位置挪好了。

「我們現在把這張沙發靠在牆邊，然後把房間裡所有的東西都搬出去，只留下椅子，各位覺得如何？」

「好啊！」

「漢斯，把這些桌子搬進吸菸室，然拿清潔機來把地毯上這些髒點清掉，接著，等等，漢斯……」喬絲喜歡發號命令指使僕人，而僕人們也樂於受命，因為她讓他們覺得大夥好像是在做一場戲劇演出。「去請媽媽和蘿拉小姐立刻過來。」

「遵命，喬絲小姐。」

喬絲轉向梅格説道：「我想試試鋼琴的聲音，以免下午有人會要求我獻唱。我們來試一下《乏味人生》這首歌。」

砰！踏踏蹡，滴答！琴聲突然變得激揚，喬絲的表情也隨之變化。她兩手緊緊握住，當媽媽和蘿拉走進來時，她用既苦澀又神祕的神情望著她們。

> 人生乏味，
> 淚珠，嘆息。
> 愛情恆變，
> 人生乏味，
> 淚珠，嘆息。
> 愛情恆變，
> 就此，別了！

P.24

唱到「別了」這兩個字時，琴聲變得更急切，喬絲的表情卻一轉，露出了燦爛的笑容，根本沒有投入在歌詞意境中。

「媽，我的嗓子很不錯吧？」她開心地問。

> 人生乏味，
> 希望頓減。
> 如夢初醒。

就在這時，紗荻打斷了她們。

「紗荻，什麼事？」

「夫人，容我打斷，廚子問你有沒有準備三明治要用的小插旗？」

「紗荻，你是説『三明治要用的小插旗』？」榭里丹夫人重覆著紗荻的話，楞楞地問道。孩子們一看到她這種表情，就知道媽媽準是忘了。

「是這樣子啊！你跟廚子說，我十分鐘之後會拿給她。」媽媽用很肯定的口氣對紗荻說。

紗荻於是退下。

媽媽很快地說道：「蘿拉，你現在和我去抽菸室，我都寫好了，寫在哪個信封袋的背面了，你幫我謄下來。梅格，你現在上樓去把你頭上的濕毛巾拿下來。喬絲，立刻奔去換衣服。還有，喬絲，你去廚房時，把我安撫一下廚子好嗎？我今天早上可怕她了。」

P.25

終於，他們在餐廳的時鐘後面找到了信封袋，樹里丹夫人不解信封袋怎會擱在那裡。

「一定是你們哪個小鬼從我的袋子裡把信封袋偷走，我明明記得很清楚的……奶油起士檸檬蛋塔……是不是你們偷走的？」

「沒錯！」

「蛋和……」樹里丹夫人把信封袋移遠些，說道：「這個字看起來像『mice』（老鼠），但不可能是 mice 的啊，難道不是嗎？」

「是 olive （橄欖）。」蘿拉轉頭往身後一望，說道。

「哦，對，是橄欖。蛋和橄欖，這種搭配聽起來滿嚇人的！」

謄完之後，蘿拉拿著旗子來到廚房，

這時看到喬絲正在安撫廚子，廚子看起來一點不可怕。

「這是我看過最精緻的三明治了！」喬絲用很驚喜的語氣說道：「大廚，你說你做了幾種三明治？十五種？」

「是十五種沒錯，喬絲。」

「恭喜你完成了，大廚。」

廚子一邊拿著長長的三明治刀把麵包皮切掉，一邊笑得合不攏嘴。

「歌啵來囉！」紗荻從食品室走出來，一邊說道。

P.26

歌啵是指奶油泡芙。歌啵最有名的產品就是奶油泡芙了，大家寧可用買的也不想自己做。

「我的好女孩，把泡芙拿過來，放在桌子上吧。」廚子發令道。

紗荻把泡芙放好之後，又走回門的那頭。當然蘿拉和喬絲已經是大女孩了，不再對泡芙這麼感興趣，但她們還是免不了讚賞幾句，說泡芙看起來實在很吸引人，太誘人啦。廚子開始動手整理泡芙，把多餘的糖霜甩掉。

「看到這個，小時候的派對回憶又剎時浮現，是吧？」蘿拉說道。

「我想是啦。我得說，泡芙看起來白白泡泡的，很柔軟。」個性實際、不喜歡沉浸於回憶之中的喬絲說。

「親愛的，你們各拿一個去吃吧，你媽媽不會發現的。」廚子柔聲細語地說。

哦，不會吧，才剛吃完早餐，就要吃這種特製的奶油泡芙，真讓人不敢領教。

然而，不一會兒，還是看到喬絲和蘿拉各自舔著自己的手指頭。她們那種專注的表情，是人在吃過奶油之後所會特有的表情。

「我們去花園，去後院那裡。我想去看工人棚子搭得怎樣了，他們是一群很好的人喔。」蘿拉建議道。

思索一下
・蘿拉和喬絲在吃奶油泡芙時，你能想像她們在想什麼嗎？
・有什麼食物會勾起你童年時的回憶？

P.27

未料門口這時圍了廚子、紗荻、歌啵的送貨人和漢斯。有事情發生了。

廚子像隻激動的母雞那樣發出「咕咕」聲；紗荻用雙掌貼住臉頰，那個動作跟牙痛很像；漢斯一臉困惑，猜想著出了什麼事；倒是那位歌啵的人，他一副很泰然的樣子。這件事情他是知道的。

「怎麼回事？發生什麼事了？」

「發生可怕的意外了！」廚子說：「死了人啦！」

「死了人了？在哪裡？怎麼會這樣？什麼時候的事？」

對於這件事，歌啵的人並不打算把它默默放在心裡頭。

「小姐，你知道下面那裡的那些小木屋

嗎？」可不知道嗎？她當然知道了。「那裡住了一個叫史考特的年輕人，他是運貨馬車的車夫。今天早上，在豪客街的一個轉角，他的馬被一個引擎聲嚇到，結果馬跳起來把他摔到地上，他撞到腦後勺，就一命嗚呼了！」

「一命嗚呼了！」蘿拉盯著歌啵的人看。

「人們把他抬起來時，他已經斷氣了。」歌啵的人頗為津津樂道地說著：「他們把他的屍體運回家時，我剛好也一路跟著來到你們這裡。」接著他對廚子說：「他留下了一個老婆和五個年幼的孩子。」

「喬絲，你跟我來。」蘿拉抓住姊姊的衣袖，拉著她穿過廚房，來到綠色門的這一邊，然後停下腳步，將身上倚在門上。

P.28

她受到驚嚇地說道：「喬絲！我們是不是要把一切都停下來？」

「把一切都停下來？蘿拉！你是指什麼？」喬絲訝異地問。

「我當然是指花園派對啦。」喬絲何必假裝聽不懂？

但喬絲露出更吃驚的表情，「把花園派對停下來？親愛的蘿拉啊，這太荒謬了！我們當然不能這樣做啊，也沒有人會要我們這樣做，太誇張了啦！」

「可是大門外面那裡有人往生了，我們也不能在這種時候舉辦花園派對啊！」

思索一下

- 蘿拉和喬絲對史考特過世的反應，你有何看法？
- 要是你，你會想怎麼做？

那樣做的確是太誇張了。小木屋位在山腳下，巷子通向他們的房子，雙方之間橫越著一條大馬路。沒錯，這兩家的距離太近了。小木屋簡陋不堪，一點也沒有資格當他們的鄰居。那是些破舊的白色小房子，菜園裡只有甘藍菜的菜梗、生病的母雞，和一些番茄罐頭；連他們煙囪裡飄出的炊煙，都是一副寒酸樣，炊煙一小塊一小塊的，不像榭里丹家的煙囪，竄出來的炊煙銀白色的好大一朵，直直地往上升騰。

巷弄裡住的是洗衣婦，還有煙囪工人、一個鞋匠，另外還住了一個房子前面掛滿小鳥籠的人。

P.29

那裡隨處可以看到小孩。榭里丹家的孩子都還很小時，是不准跑去那裡玩的，那裡的人講話很粗俗，再說也怕會染上什麼病。

等他們長大後，蘿拉和勞瑞有時候會散步走過。那裡很髒很亂，他們會嚇得趕緊出來。但人總是要四處走走、到處看看的，所以他們還是會穿越過去。

「你想想看，那個可憐的婦女要是聽到樂隊的聲音，會是怎樣的一種滋味？」蘿拉說。

喬絲開始覺得不耐煩地說：「哎呀，蘿拉！要是只要有人發生意外，就要取

消樂隊表演，那日子就很難過下去了！這件事情我和你一樣覺得很遺憾，我也很同情。」她的眼神變得很嚴厲，她盯著妹妹，那個眼神跟他們小時候吵架時的神情一模一樣，「你以為你這樣濫用同情心，就能讓那個喝醉酒的工人起死回生嗎？」她輕聲地說的道。

「喝醉酒？誰說他喝醉酒了？」蘿拉口氣兇巴巴地對喬絲說。她們在吵這種事情時，她的口氣一向如此，「我要去跟媽媽說這件事情！」

「那就去啊！」喬絲裝出咕咕地聲音說道。

P.30

「媽，我可以進你房間嗎？」蘿拉一邊說道，一邊轉開玻璃做成的大門把。

「當然可以啊，孩子。怎麼啦？發生什麼了？你的臉色是怎麼了？」榭里丹夫人從梳妝台上轉過頭來，她正在試戴一頂新帽子。

「媽，有人死了。」蘿拉開始說道。

「不是死在花園裡吧？」媽媽打斷她的話問道。

「不是，不是！」

「哦，你嚇了我一跳！」榭里丹夫人鬆了口氣。她把頭上的大帽子拿下，放在膝蓋上。

思索一下

- 榭里丹夫人為什麼鬆了一口氣？
- 你對榭里丹夫人的反應有何想法？

「媽，妳想想看。」蘿拉說道。她屏著氣，有些呼吸不上來地說著這件可怕的事情。「我們當然不應該再開派對的，對吧？媽，樂隊和客人會來，他們都會聽到的，他們也算是我們的鄰居啊！」她用懇求的語氣說。

出乎蘿拉的意外，媽媽的反應和喬絲如出一轍。更甚的是，媽媽看起來心情很好，不把蘿拉的話當一回事。

「親愛的孩子啊，運用你的常識來做判斷吧。我們不過是不小心聽到了這樁意外，如果假設對方是自然死亡——我真不曉得他們在那麼小的洞裡怎麼過生活——我們就會如期舉辦派對，不是嗎？」

P.31

對此，蘿拉無法否認，但她就是覺得這樣做很不妥當。她坐在媽媽房間裡的沙發上，捏著靠墊的邊緣。

「媽，這樣我們不是顯得很冷酷無情？」她問道。

「親愛的！」樹里丹夫人拎著帽子，起身走向蘿拉。蘿拉來不及躲，媽媽已經把帽子套到她頭上了。

「我的孩子啊！這帽子是你的，很適合你，我戴起來會太年輕了。沒想到你戴起來會這麼好看，你自己瞧瞧！」媽媽說罷，便把手持鏡拿起來。

「但是，媽媽！」蘿拉重啟話題。她把頭轉過去，不想照鏡子。

這下子，和喬絲剛剛的反應一樣，樹里丹夫人失去了耐性。

「蘿拉，你太荒謬了！」她冷冷地說道：「像他們那樣的人，是不會期待我們要去做什麼犧牲的，而且你現在這樣破壞大家的興致，一點也不仁慈！」

「我不懂啦！」蘿拉說罷就快步走出房間，回到自己的臥室。回到房間裡，出其不意、首先映入眼裡的，是鏡子裡那位美麗的女孩，她戴著一頂黑色的帽子，帽子上裝點著雛菊，繫著一條黑絲絨長緞帶。

P.32

她沒想到自己戴起來會這麼好看，難道媽媽是對的嗎？她琢磨著。這個時刻，她但願媽媽說對了。我是否真的想太多了？興許是我是想太多了。剎那間，她腦海裡閃過畫面，那個可憐的婦女，那些可憐的小孩，還有被抬進屋子裡的屍體。但這些畫面就像報紙上的圖片那樣模糊不清，缺乏真實感。她當下決定，等到派對結束後，她就會再想起這件事。目前這樣處理是最好的了。

一點半時，午餐結束。兩點半時，派對一切準備就緒。一身綠衣打扮的樂隊已經抵達現場，正在網球場上的角落裡做準備。

「親愛的！他們是不是愛青蛙愛得無法言語啦！你應該安排他們在池塘邊做演

里丹夫人的花園裡，要飛往……哪兒呢？啊，和愉快的人們相伴，大家互相握手、親吻、相視微笑，何等之幸福！

「親愛的蘿拉，你看起來真漂亮啊！」

「這帽子真適合你啊，孩子！」

「蘿拉，你看起來很有西班牙風，沒見過你這麼漂亮！」

容光煥發的蘿拉輕聲地答道：「你喝茶了嗎？要加冰淇淋嗎？這個百香果冰淇淋的口味很特別喔。」她跑向父親，央求道：「親愛的爹地，不給樂隊送點喝的過去嗎？」

這個美好的午後，就這樣再冉冉地綻放，緩緩地萎去，再慢慢地逝去。

思索一下

• 作者用了什麼樣的譬喻來形容時光的流逝？
• 你會如何形容時光？

出，並請指揮者站在中間的葉子上。」凱蒂・麥藍興奮地說道。

這時，勞瑞下班返回，他一邊揮手向他們示意，一邊走去換派對要穿的衣服。看到勞瑞，蘿拉又想起那樁意外。她想跟勞瑞說這件事，如果勞瑞也認同其他人的看法，那他們就一定都沒有錯了。她跟著勞瑞的身後走進大廳。

「勞瑞！」

「哈囉！」這時勞瑞已經走上樓梯，他回過身，一看到蘿拉，就鼓起腮幫子，瞪大眼睛瞧著她。「哇，哇，蘿拉！你看起來真美！好漂亮的帽子啊！」勞瑞說。

P.34

蘿拉小聲地說：「是嗎？」她抬眼對著勞瑞笑了笑，終究隻字未提那事件。

不久，客人開始魚貫來到，樂隊也開始演奏，雇來的服務生穿梭在房子和棚子之間。到處可見三三兩兩的人們，或四處漫步著，或俯身聞著花香，或彼此寒暄，或在草坪上穿行著。他們就像雀躍的鳥兒，在今天這個午後棲落在樹

P.35

蘿拉幫著媽媽一起送客，他們並排站在走廊旁，直到客人全部離去。

「總算結束啦，謝天謝地！蘿拉，你去把其他人找來，我們大家來杯現泡的咖啡。我好累啊！派對辦得很成功是沒錯啦，只是，這些派對，這些派對啊！你們這些小孩子怎麼非辦派對不可啊！」樹

里丹夫人説。

這時大家都已經坐在空無客人的棚子下。

「親愛的爹地，來塊三明治吧，這個旗子是我寫的喔。」

「謝啦。」榭里丹老爺大口一咬，整個三明治就都進了肚子。

「我猜你們今天都沒聽説那件可怕的意外。」老爺説道。

榭里丹夫人攤出手，説道：「親愛的，我們都聽説了。這件事還差點就讓派對開不成了，蘿拉認為我們應該把派對延期。」

「哦，媽！」蘿拉不希望別人拿這件事來消遣她。

「怎麼説這都是一件可怕的事情。那個人都結婚了，就住在我們這條巷子的下面，他留下了一個老婆，還有半打的孩子，人們是這麼説的。」榭里丹老爺説。

接著是一陣尷尬的沉默。榭里丹夫人玩著手上的杯子。可不，這是一個頗不識相的父親……

P.36

夫人突然抬眼瞧了瞧，桌子上都是沒動過的三明治、蛋糕、泡芙，等著被扔掉。她靈機一動，説：「我知道了！我們可以拿籃子來裝這些高檔的食物，送給那個可憐的女人，起碼對那些小孩子來説是難得的享受，你們同意嗎？而且她一定會把鄰居也都叫來。這麼省事的事，何樂而不為？」夫人跳起身來，説：「蘿拉，去把廚櫃上的大籃子拿過來！」

「媽，你覺得這樣做真的好嗎？」蘿拉問。

這可奇怪了，這個時候蘿拉似乎又跟大家的想法不一樣。把派對剩下的小點心送過去，那位可憐的婦女會喜歡嗎？

「當然會啊！你今天是怎麼搞的？一、兩個鐘頭之前，你還説我們應該要有同理心。」好吧！蘿拉快跑去拿來籃子裝食物，媽媽把食物堆得尖尖的。

「親愛的，你一個人拿過去吧！像你平常那樣跑下去，不，等等，把這個海芋也拿過去吧，像他們那樣階級的人，是很稀罕海芋的。」

「海芋的莖會弄髒蘿拉的裙子。」個性實際的喬絲説。

就在這時，蘿拉的裙子差點就被弄髒了。「那你帶籃子過去就行了。還有，蘿拉……，你不可以……」她媽媽一邊跟著她走出棚子，一邊説道。

P.38

「什麼，媽？」

算了，還是別提了，不需要跟孩子提這些事！「沒事，快去吧！」

思索一下
• 你想，榭里丹夫人會想跟蘿拉講什麼？
• 榭里丹夫人為什麼欲言又止？
• 把派對剩下的食物，送去給往生者的家人，你覺得妥當嗎？

蘿拉關起花園的門時，天色已經漸自暗了。有一條大狗黑影幽幽地倏忽而過，馬路反射出白光，下方低處的那些小木屋黑抹抹的一片。相對於午後時光，這個時刻顯得特別闃寂。蘿拉往山坡下跑去，朝著一個靜靜躺著的死人跑去，她不是很明白自己為何要這樣做：為什麼不能呢？她停下來半响，派對上的那些親吻、交談聲、湯匙聲、笑聲，還有草坪被踐踏後所逸出的氣味，隱約都還縈繞在她心頭，她整個腦海裡想的都是這些。好奇怪！她抬頭仰望黯淡的天空，心裡淨想著：「沒錯，派對辦得太成功了！」

P.39

這時她穿過馬路，來到灰濛陰暗的巷子口。披著披巾的婦女和戴著帽子的男人，匆匆而過。圍籬旁邊有男人在閒晃，小孩子們在門口前嬉戲。這些破舊的小木屋傳出低沉的嗡嗡聲，有些屋子透出搖曳的燈光，窗戶閃過幢幢黑影。

蘿拉低下頭，快步走著。她但願自己有披上外套，因為她這身衣服太搶眼了！還有，那頂繫著絨絲帶的大帽子，但願她戴的不是這頂帽子！人們是不是在盯著她瞧？一定是的！她真不該來這裡，這件事從頭到尾都是一場錯誤！她是不是應該趁這個時候趕快走回去？來不及了！她已經來到房子的前面，一定就是這一家了，房子外頭圍著黑壓壓的人群。在大門旁邊，有一個拿著拐杖的老嫗，她坐在一張椅子上，在一旁觀看，腳底還踩著一份報紙。

P.40

蘿拉朝屋子走去，聲音一時寂靜了下來。人們讓開路，就像她想像的那樣，這些人彷彿早就知道她會走過來。

蘿拉很緊張，她把絨絲緞帶往肩後推，向旁邊站著的一個婦女問道：「這是史考特先生的家嗎？」婦女露出詭異的笑容，應聲道：「是的，姑娘。」

快讓我脫離這一切吧！她一邊轉進小路叩門時，還一邊說著：「神啊，救救我！」讓我逃離這些人注視的眼光，或是拿個什麼東西來把我遮住，就算是拿那些婦女的披巾來把我藏住都好。她決定只要一把籃子放下，就要立刻離開，不要在那裡等著拿回空籃子！

思索一下

・走在巷子裡，蘿拉有什麼感受？她為什麼會有這些感受？
・蘿拉打算怎麼做？
・如果你是蘿拉，你會作何感想？

P.42

這時，屋子的門打開了，黑暗之中，出現一位身穿黑色衣服的嬌小婦女。

蘿拉問道：「你是史考特太太嗎？」

對方的回應讓蘿拉感到很害怕：「小姐，請進。」接著她就被關進門內，進到走廊裡了。

「不用了，我不想進去，我只是想送個籃子來而已，媽媽要我送……」蘿拉說道。

站在黑暗走廊上的嬌小婦女好像沒聽到蘿拉的話似的，不客氣地說：「小姐，請往這邊走。」蘿拉只好跟著走進去。

她進到一間破舊低矮的小廚房，廚房裡有一盞冒著煙的油燈，爐火前坐著一個婦女。

讓蘿拉進門的那位嬌小婦女說道：「愛恩！愛恩！有一位年輕的小姐來訪。」她轉身向蘿拉說道：「小姐，我是她的姊姊，你不會見怪她吧？」

「哦，當然不會！拜託不用麻煩她了，我這就要走了……」

這時，爐火前的婦女轉過臉來，她的臉有點浮腫，紅紅的，眼睛和嘴唇也是腫腫的，樣子有點嚇人。她露出不解的表情，不知道眼前怎麼會來了這個人。到底怎麼了？廚房裡怎麼會來了一個提著籃子的陌生人？這是怎麼一回事？這張可憐的臉又開始哭泣了起來。

「親愛的，好吧，由我來跟這位年輕的小姐道謝就好。」另一個婦女說道。

婦女又說了一次：「小姐，我相信你一定能見諒吧！」她的臉也是有點腫腫的，她勉強地跟蘿拉擠出笑容。

P.43

蘿拉一心只想趕快走出房子，離開這裡。她回到走廊，那裡有扇門是打開的，她直走穿過門，進到臥室，那個已經去世的男人就躺在那裡。

「你想看看他，對吧？」愛恩的姊姊說罷，便繞過蘿拉，輕輕碰了她一下，然後走到床邊。「姑娘，你不用怕。」婦人說這話時，輕柔的聲音帶著詭異。她輕輕地把布掀開，說：「他看起來就像張照片，沒什麼的，過來吧，親愛的。」

蘿拉走了過去。

那裡躺著一個年輕的男子，他睡得好熟——睡得這麼沉、這麼深，和他們離得好遠好遠。他在一個很遙遠、很靜謐的地方。他在睡夢中，無法喚醒。他閉

93

著雙眼，把頭深深地埋進枕頭裡。在緊閉的眼簾底下，他的雙眼不會看到東西，他沉湎在他的夢裡。花園派對、籃子或是蕾絲衣服，對他來説又有何意義？他已經遠遠離開這些東西了！他看起來很奇妙，很美。在人們嬉笑時，在樂隊演奏時，這個巷子裡正上演著一件奇異的事。

「快樂的……幸福的……，一切都這麼美好，」這張沉睡的臉龐如是説著，「一切，恰如所是，我別無所求。」但即使如此，你總不免要哭一場，而且她也不能沒説個幾句話就離開。蘿拉啜泣了一聲，聲音很大聲，像個小孩似的。

「請原諒我戴這頂帽子來。」她説。這次她不等愛恩的姊姊領路，逕自走出房門，穿過黑壓壓的人群，沿著小路離開。

P. 44

她走到巷口時，踫到了勞瑞。

勞瑞從黑夜中走來。「蘿拉，是你嗎？」

「是！」

「媽媽愈想愈擔心。你沒事吧？」

「很好，沒事。哦，勞瑞！」她抓住勞瑞的手臂，緊緊靠著他。

「你沒有哭吧？你哭了嗎？」她的哥哥問道。

她搖搖頭。但實際上她是哭了。

勞瑞伸手抱住她的肩膀，用溫柔疼惜的聲音説：「別哭了！是很可怕嗎？」

「不是，只是很神奇而已。勞瑞……」她話説到一半，望著哥哥，接著躊躇地説道：「生命是不是……，是不是……」她無法説明生命是怎麼一回事，但這不

要緊，哥哥能聽得懂。

「親愛的，不就是這樣嗎？」勞瑞説。

思索一下

- 蘿拉看到往生者的反應，跟你想像的差不多嗎？
- 哪裡跟你想像的一樣？哪裡又不一樣？
- 你想，蘿拉最後所想表達的對生命的想法是什麼？

六便士銅板

P.57

　　小孩子是很難摸透的。像弟奇這樣一個小不點男孩——通常是很乖巧、懂事、溫柔、聽話，對自己的年紀很敏感——他的情緒也會有變幻莫測一面，會突然毫無徵兆地變成一頭「瘋狗」，這個封號是他的姊姊們給。難道，沒有方法可以治得了他嗎？

　　「弟奇，你過來！過來，孩子，立刻過來！你沒聽到你媽在叫你嗎？弟奇！」

　　然而弟奇是無論如何也不會過來的。他當然是有聽到，而且聽得很清楚，但他只會有一種反應，那就是發出一個小小的銀鈴般笑聲，然後跑開，把自己躲起來。他會穿過沒有刈過的草坪，急急跑過柴房，往菜園那邊奔跑過去，躲在蘋果樹的樹幹後面盯著媽媽瞧，然後像隻野生動物跳上跳下的。

　　這些戲碼在下午茶時刻上演了。那個下午，史畢司太太過來陪弟奇的媽媽，他們靜靜地坐在客廳裡做針線活。孩子們當時都很乖，靜靜地吃著奶油麵包，一切都很美好。然而就在侍女在倒牛奶和

水的時候，弟奇突然抓起裝麵包用的盤子，倒扣在自己的頭上，接著又抓起切麵包用的刀子。

　　「你們看！」他大聲喊道。

P.58

　　姊姊們受到驚嚇地看著他，侍女還來不及把盤子搶過來，放麵包的盤子就已經搖搖晃晃滑落到地板上摔碎了，嚇得小女孩們驚聲尖叫。

　　「媽！你快過來看看他幹的好事！」

　　「弟奇摔破了一個很大的盤子！」

　　「媽，你快過來管管他啊！」

　　你能想像媽媽急急跑過來的樣子嗎？但她來晚了，弟奇已經跳下椅子，穿過落地窗，跑到外面的走廊上了。媽媽只能站在那裡，無計可施。

　　媽媽能拿他如何？她又不能一路追著孩子跑，穿梭在蘋果樹和梅子樹之間來追捕弟奇，那樣子太難看了。這件事不只氣人，而且很難堪，尤其是史畢司太太還在場！史畢司太太的兩個男孩是那麼乖，就坐在客廳裡陪著媽媽。

　　「很好，弟奇，我要想個方式來懲罰你。」媽媽大聲說道。

　　「我才不怕呢！」他用細細尖尖的聲音說道，然後又是一陣銀鈴般的笑聲。這個孩子的行徑太異常了！

• 你想,弟奇為什麼會有這樣的行為舉止?
• 你小時候是怎樣的一個小孩?

P.59

「哦,史畢司太太,實在很抱歉,要這樣把你一個人留在這裡。」

「班道太太,不要緊的啦。」史畢司太太用她輕輕甜甜的聲音說道。她像是對自己笑了笑地說:「這種小事情是家常便飯,只要不會造成什麼問題就好。」

「不就是弟奇嘛!」班道太太一邊莫可奈何地找著她那根唯一高檔的針,一邊說道。她對著史畢司太太把事情一股腦兒說出來,「最慘的是,我不知道要怎麼治他。只要他情緒一來,我就拿他一點辦法也沒有。」

史畢司太太睜開她淡色的眼睛,說道:「一點點辦法都沒有嗎?」

班道太太一邊拿線穿針,一邊說道:「我們是從來不打小孩的,那些女孩是用不著打的,而弟奇是這樣一個寶貝,他是獨子,怎麼說也是……」

史畢司太太放下手上的針線活,說道:「親愛的,這也難怪弟奇會有這種小小的暴走行為,我這樣說你不介意吧?孩子不打不成器,我想這就是你犯的最大錯誤。小孩子不打是不行的,親愛的,這是我的經驗。我以前也是想用比較溫和的方式,」

史畢司太太吸了一口氣,發出一些些嘶嘶的聲音,說道:「像是拿黃色的肥皂塗在男孩們的舌頭上,或是星期六時讓他們在桌子上罰站一整個下午。不過,相信我,沒有什麼方法會比把男孩交給他們的爸爸來得有效。」

聽到黃色肥皂的方法時,班道太太實著大吃一驚。然而史畢司太太卻一副稀鬆平常的樣子,她確實是覺得沒什麼大不了。

「交給他們的爸爸,那你就不親自動手囉。」班道太太說。

「我才不親自動手呢!」史畢司太太對這個想法感到震驚,「打小孩不是媽媽的工作,這是做父親的責任,再說他爸在小孩面前有威嚴多了。」

「對,這我想像得出來。」班道太太小聲地說。

史畢司太太對班道太太露出親切與鼓勵的笑容,「我的兩個小孩,他們要是天不怕地不怕,現在就會和弟奇一樣,但相反的……」

「哦,你的小孩是完美的典範!」班道太太叫道。

的確,能在大人面前安安靜靜、很有規矩的小男孩,是找不到的。去到史畢司家的客人就常會這麼說,他們甚至會覺得屋子裡沒有小孩。裡頭常常是沒有小孩沒錯。

史家的前門大廳掛了一大幅畫,畫裡頭畫了幾個心寬體胖的神父在河畔釣魚,在畫的下方擺了一條很粗的深色馬鞭,那是史畢司先生的父親的馬鞭。男孩們因為某種緣故,會選擇遠離鞭子的地方玩耍,像是去狗屋後方、工具室或是垃圾桶那邊嬉戲。

事。」弟奇的母親下定決心説道。

思索一下

• 史畢司太太的小孩，看起來快樂嗎？為什麼？

P.62

　　史畢司太太一邊將手上的活兒摺起來，緩緩呼吸，嘆口氣説道：「在孩子小的時候就管不住他們，那真是一種錯誤，一種令人傷心的錯誤，但偏偏這種錯誤會很容易犯。其實要記得的是，這對小孩來説是很不公平的。像弟奇今天下午的行為，就我來看，他是故意的，故意用這種行為來表示説：他欠打！」

　　「你是這樣想的？」班道太太是一個軟弱的嬌小婦女，這種説法讓她很訝異。

　　史畢司太太經驗老道地説：「是啊，我認為是這樣沒錯。偶而讓他們的父親好好修理他們一下，這樣你以後就會省事很多。親愛的，相信我，沒錯的。」她把又乾又冷的手放在班道太太的手上。

　　「等愛德華一回來，我就跟他談這件

P.63

　　在花園的門砰一聲關上之前，孩子們就得上床睡覺。這時，弟奇的爸爸會扛著他的腳踏車，腳步蹣跚地走上水泥階梯。他今天在辦公室裡諸事不順，搞得他一身疲憊，而且又熱又髒。

　　而這時，抱著新計畫的班道太太很興奮，親自來幫他開門。

　　「哦，愛德華，謝天謝地，你回來啦。」她叫道。

　　「怎麼啦？發生什麼事了？」愛德華一邊説著，一邊把腳踏車放下來，然後脫下帽子，他的頭上還有紅紅一圈戴帽子的痕跡。「什麼事啊？」

　　班道太太很快地説：「你來，來客廳裡。我實在無法跟你形容弟奇有多麼頑皮，這你是無法想像的──你一整天都待在辦公室裡，你無法想像像他這樣年紀的孩子，會做出什麼樣的事情。他實在太可怕了，我拿他沒轍，一點辦法也沒有。愛德華，我什麼方法都試了也沒用！」她屏息地把話説完：「剩下的唯一辦法，就是打他了──愛德華，這要由你來動手。」

　　在客廳的角落裡有一個

櫃子，櫃子最上面的架子上放著一隻吐著舌頭的棕色瓷器熊。黑暗中，這隻熊似乎在對著弟奇的爸爸嘻嘻地笑著說道：「好啊！這就是你回到家要執行的任務！」

P.65

愛德華看著瓷器熊，說道：「我到底為什麼要開始打他？我們以前沒打過他啊！」

「因為，你看不出來嗎？這是我們唯一的辦法了！這個孩子我管不住！」太太的話傾唇而出，在丈夫疲憊的頭上旋轉著，「我們請不起保母，侍女那邊又有做不完的活，而他的頑皮行為已經超乎想像。這你不懂的，愛德華，你不懂的，你整天都在辦公室裡。」

瓷器熊吐著舌頭，氣憤的聲音繼續轟炸著，愛德華消沉地坐在沙發上。

「我要用什麼打他？」他有氣無力地問。

「當然是用你的拖鞋啊！」太太說罷，便跪在地上，幫他把髒鞋子的鞋帶解開。

「愛德華，你都進到客廳了，褲圈竟然還沒　下！不是我愛說你……」她叫喊道。

「好啦，夠了。」愛德華差點沒有她推開，「把拖鞋拿給我！」

思索一下

• 愛德華回到家時，心情如何？
• 他的妻子做了哪些事，讓他變得更低落？
• 他為什麼決定要打弟奇了？

P.66

他走上樓，覺得自己像是置身在黑暗的羅網裡。這下子他想打弟奇了，是的，他想揍揍什麼的來出氣。天啊，這是什麼樣的人生！他發熱的眼睛上還有灰塵，他覺得自己的雙臂好沉重。

他推開弟奇房間的小門，這時弟奇就穿著睡衣站在地板中間。看到弟奇，愛德華一肚子火就上來。

「喂，弟奇，你知道我是為什麼事來找你的。」愛德華說。

弟奇默不作聲。

「我是來打你的。」

弟奇還是沒有反應。

「把你的睡衣拉上來！」

弟奇抬頭望著，臉都漲紅了。他小聲問道：「一定要嗎？」

「拜託，現在就拉上來！快一點！」愛德華說罷，就緊緊抓住拖鞋，往弟奇的身上用力打了三下。

「這樣你就會知道要好好聽媽媽的話了！」

弟奇站在那裡，把頭垂得低低的。

「還不快點上床！」爸爸說道。

弟奇還是沒有行動，只是用顫抖的聲音說：「爹地，我還沒有刷牙！」

「欸，你說什麼？」

弟奇抬起頭，他的嘴唇在發抖，但眼裡並沒有淚水。他沒有發出一點聲音，也沒有哭，他只是嚥著口水，靜靜地說：「爹地，我還沒有刷牙！」

P.68

看到眼前這個小臉蛋，愛德華轉過身，他不知道自己在做什麼。他跑出房間，走下樓，來到花園。天啊，看看他做了什麼事？他沿著樹籬走，身子沒在一棵梨子樹的樹影裡。他打了弟奇，用拖鞋打了自己的小兒子，他為什麼要打他？他連原因都沒搞清楚！

弟奇的爸爸抓住樹籬，呻吟了一聲。他沒有哭，沒有掉半滴淚。他要是能哭一哭或是氣一氣也好。「爹地！」他又聽到這一聲顫抖微弱的聲音，這是一聲盡在不言中的寬恕，然而，他不能原諒自己，永遠也無法原諒自己！他是孬種！是笨蛋！是畜生！這時，他想起有一次他們一起玩時，弟奇從他的膝蓋上跌落，扭傷了手腕，卻連一滴眼淚都沒有掉。他剛剛動手打的，是一個小小的英雄好漢。

思索一下

• 愛德華打了弟奇之後，心情是怎樣的？為什麼？

• 你想弟奇被打了之後，會怎麼想？

P.69

愛德華心想，這件事一定要做個處理。他快步走回屋子，上樓來到弟奇的房間。這個小男孩現在已經躺上床，他小小的頭有一半曝露在燈光下，他額頭前剪得方方的瀏海，在淡色的枕頭上看得很清楚。他直直地躺躺著，到現在都還沒哭過。愛德華把門關上，靠在門上。他想做的，就是跪在弟奇的床邊，痛哭一場，請求原諒。不過，當然他只能想不能做。他覺得難受，心裡感到刺痛。

「弟奇，你還沒睡嗎？」他輕聲說道。

「還沒，爹地。」

愛德華走過來，坐在兒子的床上，弟奇透過長長的睫毛看著他。

「沒事的，對不對？」愛德華略微低聲地說道。

「沒，爹地。」弟奇應聲道。

愛德華伸出手，小心的抓起弟奇熱哄哄的小手。

「你，不要再想剛剛發生的事情了，小人兒。你看，都結束了，都過去了，而且這種事永遠不會再發生了，你說好嗎？」他靜靜地說道。

「好，爹地。」

P.70

「兒子，所以現在要做的，就是讓心情好起來，然後笑一個！」愛德華說。他自己先擠出了一個笑容，「把這一切都忘了，好嗎？小人兒……老男孩……」

弟奇像之前一樣躺著不動，情形看起來不太妙。爸爸跳起來，走到窗前，花園裡黑漆漆一片。侍女跑到外面，把灌木叢上的白布收起來擱在手臂上。在遼闊的夜空上，金星閃爍，在黯淡的夜色下，一棵大樹的樹影娑婆搖曳著。看著眼前這一切，他摸到褲帶裡的錢。他把錢掏出來，挑出一個新的六便士銅板，走回弟奇的旁邊。

「兒子啊，這個給你，你可以買你喜歡的東西。」愛德華一邊把六便士放到弟奇的枕頭上，一邊溫柔地說道。

然而，就算這樣，就算給了一個六便士的銅板，已經發生的事情，能夠一筆勾消嗎？

思索一下
- 愛德華為什麼要給弟奇一個六便士的銅板？
- 你想弟奇會作何感想？

THE GARDEN PARTY

Page 46

5 a) T   b) F   c) F   d) T   e) T
f) T   g) F   h) F   i) T

Page 47

7 (Possible answers)
- **The Sheridan's House/Garden:** alive, sun, warm, bright, happy, perfect
- **The Workers' Cottages/Lane:** smoky, dark, poor, shadow, ugly, disgusting
  The words referring to the Sheridan's house and garden all have positive connotations, while those referring to the workers' cottages and lane have negative ones.

Page 48

8

PERSON	FACTS ABOUT THEM
1 Mr. Sheridan	*The father. Absent for most of the story.*
2 Mrs. Sheridan	*The mother. Very self-centered.*
3 Laura	The main character in the story.
4 Meg	*Laura's sister.*
5 Jose	*Laura's sister.*
6 Laurie	Works in an office with his father.
7 Kitty Maitland	*A close friend of the family; she comes to lunch.*
8 Sadie	*The maid.*
9 Cook	*The person who prepares most of the food.*
10 Hans	*He helps with odd jobs in the house.*
11 The Gardener	*He works in the garden.*
12 4 workmen	*They are getting the garden ready for the party.*
13 The florist	*He delivers flowers for the party.*
14 Godber's man	Tells about Scott's death.
15 The band	They wear green uniforms and play the music.
16 Hired waiters	*They serve food and drinks at the party.*
17 Scott	The carter who was killed in an accident.
18 Em Scott	*Scott's wife.*
19 The other woman	*Scott's wife's sister.*

Page 49 (Possible answers)

10

a) She is shy and blushes. She tries to cover up by copying her mother's voice but this makes her even more nervous.
b) She is shocked and wants to stop the party.
c) She can't understand her mother and initially doesn't look at the hat.
d) She seems tired and relaxed at the end of the party and doesn't want to be teased.
e) She feels self-conscious and out of place as she is walking to Scott's house.
f) She is nervous going into the house.
g) She feels strangely happy when she is walking home with Laurie.

11 (Possible answers)
Meg spends most of the first part of the story with a towel on her head which excuses her from speaking to the workmen and doing other things. Jose is described as "the butterfly" and is practical yet dramatic. Laura is the "artistic one"; she seems the

most sensitive and aware of what is happening around her.

12

a) She is giving her children the opportunity to prove themselves.
b) She is very self-centered and is only concerned about how the death will affect her party.
c) She feels superior to Scott and people of his social class and has no regard for their feelings.
d) She can be seen as generous when she doesn't have to make a sacrifice or compromise.

Page 50
15 a) d   b) a   c) c   d) d   e) b
f) e   g) b   h) b   i) a

Page 51 (Possible answers)
18

a) The passage from childhood into adulthood
b) Learning about life
c) Social differences
d) Social conventions
e) Discovering there is more to life than the family home.

SIXPENCE

Page 74
6 He broke the bread plate
7 c)
8 Because she doesn't want to run after him and she isn't normally very strict with him.
9

a) Soaping their tongues.
b) Making them stand on the table for the whole of Saturday afternoon.
c) Beating them. She thought beating them was best.

10 Mrs. Bendall is shocked but she hides her reaction from Mrs. Spears.
11 She has never beaten him.
12 His wife asks him to beat Dicky.

Page 75
13 The brown china bear seems to tease Mr. Bendall.
14 No, he has never beaten him before.
15 b)
16 confused and guilty
17 He remembered the time when Dicky had fallen off his father's knee and sprained his wrist and he hadn't cried.

Page 76
18

"What could she do? She couldn't chase after the child. She couldn't hunt for Dicky through the apple and plum trees. That would be too undignified. It was more than annoying; it was exasperating. Especially as Mrs. Spears, Mrs. Spears of all people, whose two boys were so good, was waiting for her in the drawingroom."
It shows how weak and easily influenced Mrs. Bendall is.

20 She is angry and anxious. She immediately orders her husband to punish Dicky and accuses him of not understanding the situation.
21 She complains because he hasn't taken them off. She is formal and concerned about appearances.

Page 77
23 (Possible answers)
a) Dicky's father staggered up the steep concrete steps.
b) He was hot, dusty, and tired out.
c) A red mark showed where the brim had pressed his head. "What's up?"
d) Edward sank into a chair.

e) "What am I to beat him with?" he said weakly.
f) He felt like a man in a dark net. And now he wanted to beat Dicky. Yes, he wanted to beat something. My God, what a life! The dust was still in his hot eyes, his arms felt heavy. *They give the impression of a tired weak man who becomes angry and frustrated.*
26 He wants to apologize to Dicky but he doesn't do it as he doesn't think it would be the correct thing to do.
27 (Possible answers)

Positive	Negative
Sensitive	Moody
Affectionate	Loses control
Sensible	Hysterical
Obedient	
Brave	
Responsible	

Page 78
29 (Possible answer)
Neither Mr. nor Mrs. Bendall usually believe in physical punishment but when Mrs. Spears challenges Mrs. Bendall's beliefs, the latter quickly changes her opinion and in turn forces her husband to do so too.
30 (Possible answer)
Mr. Bendall finds out that when he is pushed he becomes very angry and is capable of doing things he doesn't want to do. He learns to appreciate his son but he also realizes that he probably cannot undo the harm he has done.
31

Dicky	He breaks a plate.	His mother tries to discipline him and is advised by Mrs. Spears.

Mrs. Spears	Advises Mrs. Bendall on how to deal with Dicky.	She convinces Mrs. Bendall that Dicky must be beaten.
Mrs. Bendall	Forces her husband to beat Dicky.	Mr. Bendall becomes angry and does something he normally wouldn't have done.
Mr. Bendall	Beats Dicky.	He regrets this when he sees the reaction of Dicky and realizes that he didn't want to beat Dicky in the first place.

Page 79
32 (Possible answer)
There is no definite resolution though we can conclude that the harm that has been done by the beating can not be undone.
33 (Possible answer)
In *Sixpence* she chooses the brown china bear. The bear seems to be accusing and making fun of Mr. Bendall. It reflects how he feels at that moment and adds to feeling of entrapment and hopelessness.
34 (Possible answer)
a) Discipline
b) Parent-child relationships
c) How you react when your beliefs are questioned
d) Social conventions
e) Guilt

國家圖書館出版品預行編目資料

曼斯菲爾德短篇小說選 / Katherine Mansfield
著;安卡斯 譯. 一初版 . 一 [臺北市]:寂天文化,
2012.5　面;公分 .

中英對照

ISBN 978-986-184-973-7 (25K 平裝附光碟片)

1. 英語　　2. 讀本

805.18　　　　　　　　　101002382

■作者 _ Katherine Mansfield　■改寫 _ David A. Hill　■譯者 _ 安卡斯
■封面設計 _ 蔡怡柔　■主編 _ 黃鈺云　■製程管理 _ 蔡智堯　■校對 _ 陳慧莉
■出版者 _ 寂天文化事業股份有限公司　■電話 _ 02-2365-9739　■傳真 _ 02-2365-9835
■網址 _ www.icosmos.com.tw　■讀者服務 _ onlineservice@icosmos.com.tw
■出版日期 _ 2012年5月 初版一刷（250101）
■郵撥帳號 _ 1998620-0 寂天文化事業股份有限公司
■訂購金額600 （含）元以上郵資免費　■訂購金額600元以下者,請外加郵資60元
■若有破損,請寄回更換　■版權所有,請勿翻印